~DEDICATION~

To Abby:
Thanks for your love, patience,
and your toleration of my weird hours and quirky whims.

To Santino:
Balance – Order – Harmony
Thank you.

Author's Note:

I've taken many liberties with the landscape of Belfast and its waterfronts and universities, while trying to remain as accurate as possible with details that I could. More than likely, those native to Belfast, or familiar with her, will pick up these discrepancies easily. I humbly apologize for anything I wonked up, and if you're ever my way, I offer a pint of *Guinness* as recompense. On the house.

To everything there is a season.
A time to be born,
and a time to die.
Book of Ecclesiastes 3:1

Lord! What fools these mortals be.
A Midsummer Night's Dream, Shakespeare

Be careful when you fight the monsters,
lest you become one.
For when long you look into the Abyss,
the Abyss looks into you.
Friedrich Nietzsche

HIRAM GRANGE
&
the Chosen One

PART 1

Chapter One

Thursday
Belfast, Northern Ireland

He sat naked in a Sumerian Circle, cross-legged, hands draped over his knees. His thighs burned and his lower back ached. Summoning was an arduous task, not to be undertaken lightly. For weaklings, it proved fatal. Always.

He wasn't afraid. He Who Walks in White had shown him what needed to be done, had given him the means. That, and his command of the Old Tongues had grown. He'd tempered himself through pain. Made himself powerful, but that which he strove to bind was powerful, also. Perhaps more so.

Dozens of small cuts stung his chest. Three slashes on each forearm puckered red and pulpy. Delicious heat filled him. With rhythmic breaths, he harnessed the pain to fuel his will. A chalice sitting in his lap swirled with blood, spit, and urine.

Summonings carried terrible risk. Bindings, however, carried more. If he proved too weak to control the Summoned, not only would *It* destroy him, but *It* would rampage unchecked until someone intervened. *If* anyone could.

Ancient symbols powered the Circle, drawn at equidistant points on the floor around him with a fingertip dipped in the chalice's mixture. Chanting, he bathed in waves of power. He felt something coming. Soon, *It* would be here.

"Y'AI'NG'NGAH, YOG-SOTHOTH, H'E – L'GETB, FA'ITRHDOG, UAAH!" He paused. "Come, Yog-Sothoth. I bind thee with my will."

The power swelled and pushed against him. He felt *Its* mind: insistent, angry, *hungry*. "Y'AI'NG'NGAH, CYAEGHA, H'E – L'GETB, FA'ITRHDOG, UAAH! Come, Cyaegha. I bind thee with my will!"

He clenched the razor blades nestled in his palms. Fresh pain exploded from each hand as he felt blood squirt between his fingers. He absorbed the pain, brought his fists over the chalice and squeezed viscous red strings into it.

It fought him. He fought back.

"Y'AI'NG'NGAH, EIHORT, H'E—L'GETB, FA'ITRHDOG, UAAH! Come, Eihort. I bind thee, with my *will!*" He opened his eyes and focused on six glossy black-and-white photos of young women laid before him. The faces in each photo had been scratched over with large red strokes.

"Y'AI'NG'NGAH, NAGAAE, HUR DE EIHORT! Come, Nagaee, spawn of Eihort!"

On the floor before the photos lay a pewter medallion, in the shape of a great eye sprouting tentacles. It was the sigil of the Summoned. "Y'AI'NG'NGAH, M'NGALAH, Y'AI'NG'NGAH OTHUYEA, FA'ITRHDOG, UAAH! Come, Eternal One, Doom Walker! I bind thee with my will!"

He dropped the blood-smeared razor blades and began to shake. His head snapped forward and his teeth clicked. *It* lurked at the threshold. The door shivered open. He cast his will upon the six photos and the medallion before him.

"Come, one who is called Yog-Sothoth, Cyaegha, Eihort, Eternal One, and Doom Walker … I bind thee with my will! Come, harvest your brood Nagaee. Feed!"

Something tore free. He swept up the chalice, the contents of which now bubbled, and drank deeply. After a long swallow, he smiled and licked clumps off his teeth. They were coming … and they were hungry.

Erin Donahue was late. She scrambled around her flat, getting dressed for tonight's concert. If she hurried, there'd be enough time to practice. God knows she needed it. Not for the first time, she cursed Foster-Mum for the long-winded phone lecture that had made her late to begin with.

Of course, Foster-Mum could care a less. A professional music career couldn't compare to settling down and starting a family. She'd never be satisfied until Erin did so, and had spent a good two hours yakking about it over the phone.

Erin clicked through her flat on black stilettos. *Hell with it. I'm not your real daughter, anyway. Why should I listen to you?*

Men found her attractive, and her sexual appeal matched her musical one. She'd entertained *many* lovers. Most of her couplings never lasted long, but that suited her fine. Foster-Mum could go hang, for all she cared.

She stopped before a hall mirror and tugged at the black, clinging dress that normally looked stunning. Of course, Foster-Mum had yapped so long, she hadn't time to iron it before dressing. Score another notch in Foster-Mum's column for making life difficult. She huffed at the mirror's wrinkled reflection, gave her hemline a last tug, then went into the dining room to practice a few rushed sets before leaving.

Her gaze fell upon today's mail on the kitchen table. She hadn't noticed earlier, but amidst them was a small, padded manila envelope. Her address had been typed. There was no return address. Erin grabbed it, tore it open, and emptied its contents into her palm, a heavy medallion on a chain, made of dull pewter, ringed with strange symbols. In its center gazed an embossed eye, surrounded by what seemed to be tentacles or waving arms.

Erin stared. Part of her felt sickened, but another part shivered, strangely thrilled. The medallion's symbols resonated of deep, unknowable things, evoking sensations similar to those invoked by music.

"A bit odd for my tastes, but why not?" She slipped the medallion over her neck, approaching the hallway mirror for a good look. Nestled just above the swell of her breasts, it contrasted nicely with her black dress. Neither too big nor too small. She regarded herself in the mirror with a raised eyebrow. "Well ... don't I look ravishing?" With a playful swish of her bobbed hair, she turned away. Time to practice.

The medallion felt warm against her skin. She breathed so heavily from rushing around that the rise and fall of her chest made it seem as if the medallion throbbed of its own accord.

She'd been struggling to find her rhythm for twenty minutes, playing with one eye on her sheet music, the other on the clock, when her throat tickled mid-note and the trumpet uttered a metallic squeak. She tried to continue, but the tickle exploded into a full-blown cough.

She jerked the trumpet away. Hand over mouth, Erin coughed, her body bent by sudden gut-wrenching spasms. With each hack, saliva filled her mouth. Her face burned.

Dammit! I'm not missing this concert! Jan will have my head!

Another cough. The tickling subsided. She remained bent over for several seconds, savoring the sudden rush of peace. Then she opened her eyes. Blood covered her hand. She tasted a copper-saltiness. Her stomach froze as she looked in the mirror.

Thick blood covered her lips. Something small and white wriggled at the corner of her mouth. Dazed, she wiped it and touched something slick and wet. When she pulled her hand away, it was coated in red—almost candy-apple red, she thought—and in her palm shivered the thing she'd seen on her face; a white *worm*. Revulsion filled her. It had come from *inside* her. *It* had caused the tickling.

Horrified, she flung the thing away, but almost immediately her coughing resumed, more violently than before. She doubled over again, but this time didn't bother covering her mouth. She spewed bloody clots, which painted the floor with bright red starfish patterns. She felt a liquid *coiling* inside. Her guts squirmed.

She looked at her trumpet's mouthpiece and whimpered. Blood dripped from it. She'd bled from her mouth while playing and hadn't noticed. Her mind teetered when she saw worms poke their heads from the mouthpiece. She gagged, threw the trumpet away, and staggered towards the kitchen garbage to vomit.

With a rocking leap, the trash bin jerked and she skidded to a halt. A pregnant quiet filled the room. The lid flipped up and down. Something inside batted it, almost playfully, as if taunting her. It flipped up and down again; opening and closing. She jerked every time.

The medallion burned against her skin.

The lid flipped open again, but this time something caught it from inside, held it open a crack. Maggots poured out and down the can, to the floor, a blanketing army of whiteness swarming towards her. She swayed as they piled around her feet and squirmed up her ankles.

She gazed blearily at the garbage can, lid still open a crack, and saw eyes blinking in the can's darkness. As the maggots burrowed through her stockings and then skin, squid-like tentacles curled over the can's edge and flicked the air. She stared, mesmerized as fleshy arms slowly unfurled.

Something heavy and slick rose from the garbage can. Eyes glittered. She screamed as it tumbled from the can, bounced off the floor and flew at her, tentacles weaving, eyes blinking … mouths puckering.

The man relaxed. It was done. Great pleasure suffused him, for coming soon was the destruction of *Hiram Grange*.

Chapter Two

It didn't matter how hard Hiram ran, he could never reach Sadie in time. As his feet pounded against the sidewalk, black hounds swarmed over her, pulled her down. Onyx teeth tore her open as she screamed.

"Sadie!"

He reached for the Webley, his fingers feeling nothing but the cold, flimsy leather of his shoulder holster, because ...

Something screeched behind him. Hiram spun about, now in his parents' bedroom, and saw his mother rising gracefully from her ruined cello. She turned and put the Webley—his father's Webley, the same gun that later claimed Sadie—to her head. As Hiram struggled, his feet mired in blood, he heard:

"Damn you, Hiram. Damn you to hell."

His mother pulled the trigger. The side of her head blew away in wet chunks.

Sadie screamed. His mother screamed. He tried to save them, but the thickening blood pooled at his feet, rose past his ankles, and held him fast while their cries tore into his soul. Sadie screamed, his mother screamed and he screamed, because they were all one—joined forever in torment, in the Abyss. They all screamed, over and over.

Hiram awoke. He felt coated in slime. For a moment, he thought he *was* in the Abyss, lost forever in darkness.

He couldn't breathe.

"Hey! What the 'ell are ya doin'? Pitchin' a fit?"

Hiram inhaled. He massaged his chest, tried to slow his heart. Perspiration-soaked clothes stuck to his chilled skin.

"Hey! Ya alright back there?"

It rushed back. He was bound for London's Heathrow Airport, on the way to Northern Ireland and his next assignment. He'd fallen asleep in the cab. Blinking, he looked up. Pin-prick eyes glared at him in the rearview mirror. "Well?"

Hiram didn't reply. He closed his eyes and ran through a meditation cycle he had learned from monks in Cambodia years ago, when he'd been hunting a jungle daemon in the village of Sang-Li. Slowly the nightmare faded. He pushed the darkness back into its little box.

Damn you, Hiram!

"I'm fine. Bloody marvelous, really."

The driver focused on the road. Hiram gazed out the window and tried to stop the darkness from morphing into thousands of screaming faces; tried to stop seeing Sadie's and his mother's among them.

The door loomed at the end of a dark hall. Something waited there, but she couldn't reach it. Otherworldly cries chilled her spine. She ran faster. Her lungs burned, heart hammered, as something powerful built within ...

But she couldn't get any closer. If she could just get there, open it and run through, she'd be safe. At the last moment, her fingers brushed the doorknob, when something yanked her back into the darkness ...

Therese Fitzgerald bolted upright and stifled a scream. Her legs twisted in sweaty bed sheets. The couch she woke on felt damp, cold. Throwing off the sheets, she sat up and cupped her face in her hands. She hadn't had that nightmare in months, not since meeting Reggie. Why was it back?

Because you and Reggie are quits, love. Makes sense, right?

What a bitch.

She ran a trembling hand through her long, blond hair, stood up and approached Cassie's street-side window. Cassie was a friend from University who'd graduated last year. They'd kept in touch, conversing often over lunch or coffee. After her blow-up with Reggie this afternoon, she hadn't had anyone to talk with. Even after three years at University, she'd made few friends.

Cassie was one of them, so Therese had rung her up. Cassie invited her to spend the night. Relieved, Therese accepted the offer. It provided a brief sanctuary, but didn't change the fact she and Reggie were through.

She sighed. As she leaned on the cool glass of the window, she played with a small charm on her bracelet, no bigger than her thumb. It was round, with an upraised slash through it, much like a lightning bolt. One side of the bolt had been engraved with a small quill and book, the other embedded with three small crystals: red, white, and blue. Found on a chain around her neck when she was left at an orphanage just outside Glen Finen, it was the only proof that she'd ever had any family. A nun had kept it until Therese grew older.

She'd stayed at that orphanage until age ten. After that, the system shuffled her from foster home to foster home until she turned eighteen. Though it sounded trite, at least she'd always had the charm. On lonely nights, it reminded her that, even as she'd been given up, *someone* had cared.

Then came Reggie. Sweet, handsome in a rugged way, he wasn't a college student but a steel worker. His innocence had attracted Therese. To her, the unassuming Reggie seemed perfect.

Of course, she hadn't foreseen his insecurities, or imagined he'd become so possessive. Lately, their fights had worsened, and even though he always apologized with wine and flowers, it wasn't long before something new set him off.

The night's chill seeped through the glass. Her thin shirt and boxers poor defense against the cold, Therese hugged herself. She didn't step away from the window, however. She loved looking at the city lights burning against the darkness.

Today's row with Reggie had been terrible. She kept an off-campus post office box for her art correspondence, and Reggie often fetched the mail when he visited. She'd received a very strange package today, containing an odd-looking medallion on a chain. It had no return address or note. Of course, Reggie had assumed it was a gift from a secret lover.

She'd thought the medallion repulsive. Ringed with strange symbols, in the center leered a gigantic eye surrounded by squiggles that she'd assumed were tentacles. Why anyone would send her such a thing, or how it could be thought a clandestine gift of passion, she hadn't the faintest idea. She'd refused to touch it, called Reggie an idiot, and he'd stuffed it into his pocket and stormed out, after coming all the way into town to do her a favor by taking an old rug to the shop because she was too busy. She felt bad about that, but what could she do?

She sighed. It might be time to kick Reggie off, unless he gave her an absolutely fantastic reason why she shouldn't.

That wasn't impossible, of course. She'd forgiven him several times before, and she couldn't deny her need for companionship. However, if it came down to it, she could do without him, because of her painting. Painting made her feel alive, made her feel like she could touch something more real than this world. Since her first brush stroke at age twelve, painting had consumed her life, and quite frankly ... Reggie couldn't compare. He knew it, too. Hence the fights.

Often, however, painting was difficult, sometimes frightening, especially when she painted her dreams and nightmares. In a moment crystallized in memory, she recalled the first time she'd dreamed of that dark hallway and door, and the painting she'd made of them. That hadn't been so bad. It had been cathartic, even, because until now, the dream had stayed away.

Of course, there was also the painting from two months ago, one of such horrible purpose she'd thrown a cloth over it, pushed it in the corner, and forgotten it. She didn't want to think about that, though. Not at all.

She sighed. Reggie would be a loss, but she could live without him. Painting, however, wasn't enough. Things were changing. She needed more, and that was probably the real reason for the nightmare's return. She needed something and was running towards it, but she had no idea what it was.

Yawning as exhaustion tugged her eyelids, Therese returned to the couch, lay down and wrapped herself up in the sofa's cardigan instead of the sweat-dampened sheets. She fell asleep and dreamed of doors and hallways, and a painting she wanted to forget.

Chapter Three

Friday Night

As Bach's *Toccata and Fugue* wavered through the agency's safe house in Belfast, Hiram's well-oiled routine carried him through his fatigue. What little sleep he'd gotten had been haunted by the ever-more frequent nightmares of …

No. Not that. Not now.

Hiram briefly assessed the room. It smelled musty, with faded yellow wallpaper peeling in places and old, thin carpeting, but it looked acceptable enough. It wasn't his Airstream trailer, his home, but it would suffice. As usual, most needs had been provided for. Dinner had been waiting: a serving of "Angels on Horseback," which consisted of delicately marinated and stewed oysters wrapped in tangy strips of bacon, all placed on thick slabs of hot, buttered Irish Beer Bread. He'd enjoyed a chilled bottle of Pinot Noir with it. Though not absinthe, as a side it had served. Soon, however, he'd need to find some real refreshment.

He swept up the Webley from the clothes bureau, engaged the barrel catch and inspected the cylinder for debris, ignoring the spent shell—the suicide shell. Finding nothing, he spun the cylinder. When it stopped turning, he took a few cartridges from the bureau and loaded the remaining chambers except the one with the hand-scored round. Finished, he snapped the Webley shut and secured it in his shoulder holster. His personal satchel sat on the bureau also, filled with the mystical odds and ends he employed as needed: various mind-enhancing drugs, lime salt and chalk, pentacles and crosses, small vials of consecrated water, other alchemical materials.

He straightened and regarded himself in the bureau's mirror. His bony, too-long limbs and lanky frame would never properly fit the suit he wore, his father's suit, but still he adjusted his jacket with ineffective tugs on both lapels, then pulled at his waistcoat, trying to align the buttons with his belt buckle. Failing miserably, he shook his head and frowned at his reflection. Blue eyes stared back at thin lips and prominent cheekbones, set against a pallid complexion, but these features paled in comparison to his nose—an overgrown, hawkish mass.

"Bloody hell. I'm balding." With his fingers, he vainly brushed loose strands of oily black hair over his receding hairline. Giving up, Hiram turned and approached a recliner in front of which sat a combination television/VCR. For this assignment, a tape had been left. He'd study then destroy it.

Hiram sat awkwardly in the low-slung recliner and lit the Presbyterian mixture in his briarwood pipe. At least the agency had remembered to supply one of the truly important things. Now slightly more relaxed, he took up an old remote from the chair's armrest, turned on the television, and pressed 'Play.' Static resolved into the smiling portrait of Mrs. Bothwell.

"*Good evening, Hiram. I hope your flight was relaxing, and that all is in order. All your basic supplies should be there, though an additional shipment is still in transit. Never fear, it will reach you shortly.*" The image paused, glanced downwards. Papers ruffled. When it looked up again, its kindly expression had sobered. "*Last night, our analysts detected enormous spikes of electromagnetic activity in Belfast, Northern Ireland, which have continued into this evening. Since then, we've gathered some disturbing police reports. Five young women were slain last night, brutally killed—disemboweled, really—within a three mile radius of one another. One of them was found not far from you, in an alley off Patchett Street. No connections have been found between them except this: they were raised in either state homes or orphanages. Odd, but we don't know what that means, yet.*

"*EM scans place the confluence somewhere in the University Quarter of South Belfast, the main campus for Queen's University. There appears to be a talismanic element to this confluence. Thanks to an informant in the local PSNI, we learned that each victim was found with the following medallion.*"

Bothwell's face was replaced by said medallion. Hiram paused the video and studied the archaic symbols ringing its edges. In the center: a gigantic eye, ringed by tentacles. He clicked 'Play.'

"*After extensive research, we determined the glyphs to be either Sumerian or Early Babylonian. The findings are ... disturbing.*" Something cold bloomed in Bothwell's eyes. Whatever she'd learned, it had unnerved her. "*According to several ancient texts, most importantly the Necronomicon—on loan from Miskatonic University—the sigil represents an ancient god notorious for its hunger. Many stories call it a shapeshifter, changeling, manikin, false man. Other stories believe it an infestation or plague. It has many different names. Yog-Sothoth is one. The most popular, however: the Tanara'ri.*

"*All the texts indicate an extensive summoning ritual, but no particular artifact is mentioned. This makes things more difficult. The confluence's source could be a talisman or a conduit. As such, a pocket EM scanner has been included in your supplies. I know you're uncomfortable with technology, Hiram, but in this case, you'll have to make do.*"

"At least you didn't send me a cell phone. Can't stand those things."

"*There's something else. Based on the stories, this creature has been summoned numerous times. Most often during war. Not long after, both sides mysteriously vanish from recorded history.*" A pause. "*The implications are clear.*"

"Indeed. This could go to hell very quickly."

"*Your objective, of course, is to either find the summoning talisman and destroy it, or eliminate the confluence's conduit, thus breaking the binding and banishing the Tanara'ri.*"

Bothwell's image paused on the screen. With a flash of insight,

Hiram suspected the Tanara'ri hadn't unnerved her as much as something else.

"*One last note. We also detected faint quantum fluctuations at all the crime scenes.*"

Hiram sat back. A chill crept up his spine. "You've got to be kidding me. Kali's tit, *please* say you're kidding."

"*We need to assume THEY'RE involved. We'll ignore them as usual, and hope they ignore us. However, be on your guard. They're not to be trusted, no matter what.*"

"Oh, hell. Hell, hell, *hell*." Hiram leaned forward and covered his face. "Faeries. I *hate* faeries."

Chapter Four

"Please, Therese. Can't we at least talk about it?"

"*Reggie. We've been over this so many times.*"

Reggie winced as he trotted through the cold wind. He didn't have an answer for that, did he? It was just how he was built. When he looked in the mirror, he never measured up. Before, it hadn't mattered. He'd nothing much to lose. Then came Therese. Suddenly, a steel mill jockey like himself was dating a beautiful college student and artist. At first it had been bliss, but lately all he could do was worry he might lose her to someone better.

The irony? He was driving her away.

"Please. Give me another chance. If we can't sort it out, you can tell me to piss off, and I'll go away."

"*Reggie ...*" A pause. "*Fine. Where should we meet?*"

Reggie's heart skipped. "Maybe *Jimmy's*, down by Tiger's Bay? If it's too packed, we could slip out to that all-night place down the street—the *Skylark*?—and grab a bite."

"*Fine. I'm at* The Hub, *but I've no cash left. I'll have to walk. Take me twenty minutes. You'd better be buying, boyo.*"

"You bet. Thanks, Therese. You won't regret this, I promise."

"*Sure. See you there.*" The cell clicked off.

"Right, then ..." he mumbled, disappointed by her abruptness. "Love you too." He stuffed the cell into his pocket and wondered how to convince Therese to forgive him. The whole thing was his fault, really. If only he hadn't acted like such an ass.

Reggie paused at an intersection haloed by the dull-orange glow of a street lamp. The thought of losing Therese soured his stomach. He wished that stupid medallion had never come in the mail. Maybe none of this would've happened. From his pocket he pulled the padded envelope containing the necklace and its charm. He shook it into his open palm. It felt oddly warm. Holding its chain, Reggie could see Therese's point. Damn thing *was* ugly. Who'd send it to a lover?

As it swayed on its chain, an odd compulsion urged him to wear it. Why?

He shrugged. Why the hell not? He slipped the chain around his neck, the warm metal disk settling against his chest. He looked down at the manila packaging in his hands. Things were so much clearer in retrospect. If it had been a gift, wouldn't it have been wrapped?

He kicked the curb. "Idiot."

"Now, now. Why would such a sweet thing like yerself be talkin' so?"

Reggie straightened. The silken voice came from an alley he'd just passed. Retracing his steps, he found a young woman leaning against a dingy red brick wall. She wore a ragged, buttoned up fur coat. Long, creamy-white legs ended in slut-red pumps.

She smiled and devoured him with bright eyes. Red lips smirked on a full face framed by thick, unruly brown locks.

"Uhm ... hello. Who are *you*?"

The woman smiled, all white teeth. "Your dreams come true, love."

Therese wobbled as she walked in the night. *The Hub* was far from the city's center, and she felt conflicted: glad for the quiet, unnerved by her isolation. Her anxiety got the best of her and she quickened her pace.

It didn't help that she'd downed three—four?—shots of *Smirnoff* with Cassie and her friends at some ridiculous club over in Chester.

Then, of all the things, *Reggie* had called. Unbelievably, she'd agreed to meet him so he could plead his case. Sighing, she brushed several hairs back from her flushed but cold face. Maybe she should just go home, forget Reggie. He'd be upset, but he'd survive.

She kept walking. Life would be much simpler if she ditched. Of course, her life had never been simple. Why start now?

"S'a bleedin' shame a young man like yerself should spend such a cold night alone." The hooker cocked her head and raised a carefully penciled eyebrow.

Reggie paused. He'd never shagged a hooker before. "I suppose." He stepped into the alley for a better look.

The whore lifted her chin, as if in subtle challenge. "Well? Anythin' *I* can do to make the blues go 'way?"

Guilt burned inside him, but Reggie couldn't help staring. She looked striking, alabaster skin pearlescent, pouting lips full and generous. He felt disloyal, but his heart pounded. So did his pants.

"I dunno. I've never …"

"Well, I've plenty of suggestions, lolly. *Loads.*" She sauntered into the streetlight's glare. She had high cheekbones, and under the fur coat lurked possibly the biggest breasts he'd ever seen. They rose and fell as she breathed.

She placed a hand on his chest and smiled, red lips shining. *Almost like blood.* Her hand felt warm. Waves of pleasurable heat flowed through him. He followed the hand's movement down his chest with an entranced gaze, mesmerized as she unzipped his coat. She reached inside and flipped loose one shirt button after another. "I … wh-what would … it cost? I'm not flush, love …"

She pursed her lips, snagged his belt buckle and pulled him

close. Her hot breath tickled his ear. "Not much, dear … just your bloody *heart.*"

Reggie's guilty lust disappeared. He pulled back and frowned. This had been a very bad idea. "What the …" His stomach lurched as a worm wriggled from the corner of the hooker's mouth. "*Oh, hell!*"

She smiled and gulped it down. "Mmmm. Now that's a fine treat, love."

Reggie gagged. Maggots streamed from her mouth and wriggled from her nostrils. In his sickened delirium, he imagined them craning their heads and hissing at him.

She shrugged off her coat. "Give us a kiss!"

Reggie screamed at what he saw: a bloated body with oozing skin, swarming with writhing maggots. Thick tentacles squirmed under the jacket. Their tips licked the air …

Reggie tried to break free, but he was too slow. Fleshy ropes wrapped around his arms and legs. He flailed while *It* dragged him to an oily breast. Before he could scream again, a thick, eel-like tongue plunged between his lips and forced his jaws open. The smell of rot filled his nostrils and he gagged as worms poured down his throat. Thousands of tiny, hungry mouths ate at his insides.

As he died, his cell jangled Therese's ring-tone.

Chapter Five

Television off, Hiram rubbed the bridge of his nose.

Damn. Of all the things. Faeries. Bloody smug bastards. I HATE them.

The Faerie were neither of the corporeal nor of the Abyss. No one knew much about them, except that they were intimately connected to the Veil. Encounters had been few, uneasy and guarded. From their limited interaction, however, one thing seemed clear: the Faerie considered themselves vastly superior to humans.

"They treat us like bloody children. *Shit*. I don't need this."

He rose and circled the room. He couldn't stay in. Normally safe house walls offered comfort. Tonight, however, they felt suffocating. Stopping at the bureau, he secured his Pritchard bayonet in its sheathe at his back and pocketed his father's briarwood pipe. Perhaps a bit more of the Presbyterian and a walk would clear his head. Besides, he had an idea. Certainly Bothwell couldn't be mistaken in her assessment of the confluence, but it wouldn't hurt to confirm certain details. According to the tape, one of the crime scenes wasn't far from here. Analyzing the scene might not produce anything useful, but it'd keep his mind off the Faerie. And Sadie …

No. Stop it. Right now.

He gathered the necessary materials from his satchel, turned and regarded the flickering candle on the bureau that paid homage to his cherished 8x10 of Jodie Foster. Not even her normally soothing profile could calm these frazzled nerves. The worst part? He felt so keyed up, he probably wouldn't enjoy his nightly constitutional. A tragedy indeed.

He liked to think that, wherever she was, Jodie shed a tear.

T' herese clicked her cell shut and sighed. Squirming on a rough, cracked-leather bar stool, she rubbed the charm on her bracelet to keep her hands from calling Reggie again. She'd gotten nothing but voice mail four times now. She couldn't help thinking maybe he'd changed his mind and gone home. In a way she felt cheated. If anything, *she* should be ditching *him* while he called *her* every ten minutes.

She bit her lip, tapping the pitted bar with a fingernail. He was a free man, and could do as he pleased. She'd freed him, after all.

Licking dry lips, she wished she could afford another shot.

T' eeth clamped on his pipe, Hiram forced himself to ignore the open sky. It helped that Belfast's waterfront at Tiger's Bay closed in tight around him. It maintained the illusion that he was boxed in, rather than out in the unprotected open.

Damn Faerie. They watched. Observed. Sat on their collective, pixie-dust asses while people died. People like Sadie. *Sanctimonious, voyeuristic bastards.*

Fatigue pulled at him. He should've retired for the night. Kali knew he needed the shut-eye. A deep part of him feared sleep, however. He knew the moment he closed his eyes, he'd again be tortured by nightmares of Sadie and his mother.

Sadie had died by his own hands. No matter how he'd been

manipulated or used, there was no denying it. If they'd never met, or he'd never allowed her access, indulging her by accepting her attentions … perhaps she'd still be alive.

He pushed these thoughts away and glanced up at the street sign, saw he'd reached Patchett Street. Sure enough, across the way sat the alley in which one of the five girls had been killed. Yellow tape closed it off. Not watch-guards. Most likely, the local Police Service believed no more evidence remained.

They were wrong.

Deflecting thoughts of Sadie and their unborn child, he drew on his pipe. The Presbyterian blunted the jagged edges of his turmoil. He trotted across the empty street, slipped under the tape and into the alley. Squatting, he brushed the cold, damp asphalt with his fingertips, detecting faint psychic vibrations of turbulent death. A veiled stain, left behind by great emotional and physical torment.

He needed to know more. Fortunately, he came prepared.

Unfortunately, it involved magic. More like mundane spell casting, really. He loathed magic, but he'd no room for personal preferences. Abyss-bound had been misclassified before. Often, even the most brilliant minds misinterpreted vague, ancient texts. Most likely, Bothwell hadn't. But *she* wasn't the one dancing on the razor's edge. He had to know for sure.

He reached into his pocket, withdrew a pouch of lime salt, along with lime chalk. With that, he drew a pyramid with an eye inside—the All-Seeing Eye—then circled it. Around that, he drew nine smaller versions that intersected with each other across the larger pyramid diagonally.

He tipped the pouch open and sifted the salt around the circle, careful not to cover the small sigils. He felt a small measure of comfort that this spell was so utilitarian. It could hardly be counted as magic, really. Most spells were only ancient methods of accessing the Veil, developed by long forgotten peoples, nothing more than pseudoscientific, alchemical formulas blending elemental science and the supernatural in esoteric ways.

No one really understood how it worked. He likened it to operating a car or computer without understand its inner mechanics. He turned the key, hit the gas, saw the results, but didn't really understand why. That's what unsettled him most; that, and he considered it lazy. He preferred doing things with his own two hands. Right now, it couldn't be helped. Magic—like silver, hawthorne stakes or consecrated water—was simply another tool at his disposal.

He put the salt down and removed a small tin from his pocket. Inside nestled dozens of chewable mescaline tablets measured to small doses. They brought users to a higher state of awareness, flooding the pineal gland of the brain with melanin. In theory, this connected him to the electromagnetic fields all around him, opening what the Ancients had called "the third eye."

He inhaled deeply, removed his pipe, then pinched a tablet from the tin and placed it under his tongue. It tasted bitter … like almonds or cyanide. From his pocket came an old matchbook from the *UberNacht*. Morbidly ironic, considering its demise.

The mescaline dissolved under his tongue. He lit a match, then closed his eyes.

Everything left a psychic soul print. An electromagnetic trace. When the mescaline activated his pineal gland, his "third eye" would open and show him these traces. The All-Seeing Eye served as a focusing agent. Lighting the lime-salt proved an elemental catalyst that opened a conduit between him and any ambient electromagnetic energy.

He felt it. Everything slowed. His heart thundered. Re-opening his eyes, he detected silvery wisps that crept and slithered, puffs of eldritch vapor clinging to the walls and ground.

"Posluzitelj mene, istina, i osuisetluti." *Serve me, truth. Illuminate.* He tossed the match onto the salt.

White-blue flames flared and poured down the alley, liquid fire that touched everything, burned nothing. In them, thousands of faces swirled. Bluish ghosts leapt and crawled. So many traces of people long since gone: pedestrians, vagrants, hookers and their johns, constables, shopkeepers, thugs, street children. The third eye showed him surging ghosts, both distant and near. One by one they winked out, the oldest fading, fresher traces taking more defined shape. The mists swirled, convulsed, finally coalesced into a solid image. Wisps of energy became arms, legs, bodies—forming into glowing still life etched in cold, ghostly blue.

A young woman stumbling backwards, hands upraised. What looked like a boy—but was not—stepping from behind a dumpster. Though the cloudy-blue image lacked detail, the boy's midsection appeared a mass of twisted flesh, glittering with inhuman eyes.

The image flickered. The mescaline wore off. The shimmering vista dissipated, leaving only a dark alley. Hiram rocked back on his heels. "Damn." The odds of Bothwell being mistaken were slight, indeed.

He needed to think. Sort things out. A bar. A good, stiff drink or three. Remembering a place the airport cabbie had mentioned, Hiram collected his things and set off.

Chapter Six

The place called Jimmy's looked nearly empty, its only patron a young woman seated at the bar, facing away from him. She didn't look up as he passed. A large man with thick arms swabbed the bar with a dirty towel. "Closin' soon. Last call's 'bout an hour."

"That'll suit. Want to raise my feet for a spot." He nodded at a table in the shadows at the back of the room. "A pint of *Guinness* and a *Bushmills* neat, mate."

"Aye. *JENNIE!*"

Hiram turned and threaded through tables to one he wanted. He sat down, leaned back and rested his head against the wall, closed his eyes. Instead of his mission, as always, there loomed Sadie. He didn't know how to make her go away. Kali knew he'd tried. He'd drowned himself in absinthe, opium, assorted other liquors and pills, yet Sadie's face—pale, thin, slightly elfin and entrancing—still begged for salvation.

There had been girls after Sadie. Pretty little things with black lips, plaid schoolgirl skirts, studded collars. They hadn't helped. Sadie called to him still. Whispering in his ear while he worked, knocking on his brain as he slept. Though he'd never bedded Sadie, every girl since had worn her face.

He opened his eyes and dropped his hands into his lap. "Ridiculous. She was nothing. Just another tart, that's all."

Really? All those Jodie Foster collages at home? The gifts from Sadie? Those are nothing, eh?

"Of course. Foolish testaments of a childish infatuation, nothing more."

"Yer pint and a *Black Bush*. That it?"

Hiram looked up and grimaced. Jennie was short, portly, with a crooked nose. "Quite." Jennie—apparently sensing his dislike—scurried off. Satisfied to be alone again, he ignored all sensibilities and drained the deep amber whiskey in one go, relishing its smooth warmth. Staring at the frothing tan head of his *Guinness*, Hiram wondered how many pints it'd take tonight to dull the jagged holes inside him.

aybe she should go home. It was clear Reggie wasn't coming. It'd been over an hour, and he still hadn't answered his cell. She felt tired, and a headache throbbed through her buzz.

That was it, then. She was free. It sucked that she was alone again, but she'd manage—resurgent nightmares or not. She leaned forward, ready to leave. Before she could, however, strong hands gently grasped her shoulders, fingers probing tenderly into that meaty place just below the neck that always ached when she was tired. A strange sensation ran through her; oddly thrilling yet depressing: Reggie had made it after all.

She settled down. "What the *hell*, Reggie? I've been waiting forever."

"Sorry, love." His voice sounded strange. "Got caught up with something."

"Caught up? At this time of night? With what?"

There was no answer as Reggie continued to massage. A stray finger dug painfully, and she winced. "*Watch* it, Regg. You always get too carried away ..."

The barest suggestion of ... *something* ... felt its way onto her neck. She turned and almost gagged when she saw a thick maggot curl off Reggie's hand and onto her skin.

"*Oh, hell ... Reggie ...!*"

His fingers clenched. Her heart sped. She wrenched around and saw what remained of Reggie Bannister. Time froze, until a thick, bloated maggot squirmed from his left nostril. Smiling, he revealed a mouthful of worms. "*Hello, Therese. Good to see you, love.*"

Therese screamed and tried to flee, but her clumsy legs twisted. She toppled to the floor, hard. Somehow she rolled onto her back and scrambled away. Reggie loomed over her, awful face smiling. Waggling a pale finger, he made a muffled tsk-tsk. "*Now, now. Running away, are we? That's a bad girl, Therese.*"

She skittered backwards into a wall and ran out of room. Briefly, she imagined leaping to her feet and running, but fear short-circuited her brain's frenzied messages to her limbs. As Reggie slurped, leaving slime-encrusted maggots on his chin, she screamed.

Chapter Seven

Hiram's chair slammed down, causing him to drop his pint. "Ridiculous. Can't a fellow take time to ..."

Another tortured scream. Quickly Hiram found the source: a man advanced upon the young woman from the bar. Fear painted her face.

Hiram frowned. Something felt wrong. The barkeep rushed the attacker, only to be swatted aside like a paper doll, with nary a break in the man's stride. Something felt *very* wrong.

"Damn!" Hiram bolted from his chair. Closing the distance in bounding strides, he grabbed the stranger's shoulders, slammed his head into one of the pub's columns, then flung him against the bar. He drew the Webley, only to have it batted away. He ducked as a punch sailed over him and struck the column, which shook and splintered. Spinning, he unsheathed his trusty Pritchard and slashed at his attacker's ribs.

He was rewarded with an ululating howl and the scent of charred flesh. Years ago, the 8.3-inch steel blade had been blessed by Hopi medicine men as thanks for saving a Nevada reservation menaced by skin-walkers. He'd give them this much; the Native Americans knew their alchemy. The cold steel of the bayonet contained enough iron to hurt Abyss-walkers, but the blessing gave it an extra kick.

Something burned Hiram's hand. Glancing down, he saw his blade coated with dozens of writhing white maggots sizzling under Hopi magic. Fleeing, one of them had oozed onto his hand and was burrowing into his skin.

"Hell!" Hiram dislodged it, but not before it took a chunk of flesh with it. If even *one* had gotten *inside him* ...

He looked up, his stomach clenching at the sight of the wound he'd scored along the beast's abdomen. Masses of white maggots teemed inside red, dripping tissue that sealed itself liked putty.

He recalled the vision in the alley.

Tanara'ri.

They circled. Hiram faced the bar; *It* stood in his way. How to beat this thing? Elemental fire always proved a good bet. Of course, he'd left his most effective supplies at the safe house; the Webley lay out of reach. He had an old lighter for his pipe, nothing more.

Regular fire would *damage* necrotic tissue just fine, however. Hiram scanned the bar. Behind it, shelves of sparkling, multi-colored bottles reached to the ceiling, everything from *Glen Fiddich* to Bourbon to *Beefeater*. His lighter and liquor equaled fire. One problem: this *thing* blocked his path.

He brandished his blade. The Tanara'ri hissed and lunged, outstretched hands dissolving. Hiram bent and sliced a whistling figure eight, severing both of the creature's hands at the wrists. They exploded into gore. Maggots rained everywhere. Hiram spun, unfortunately *away* from the bar and its liquor treasure trove. *Fire, dammit! I need fire!*

The Tanara'ri screeched and shook ragged stumps smoldering with Hopi magic. Hands reforming, it howled and attacked again. Hiram twisted, sidestepped, ducked, tried to find an opening to the bar. He cut away large swaths of necrotic tissue, but still the Tanara'ri blocked his every turn.

Hiram's thighs and calves ached. He needed fire, *now*.

It happened quickly. Looking for a hole to slip through to the bar and its liquor stores, Hiram overcompensated and stumbled. The thing's belly split open and something wriggled out. As Hiram scrambled for footing, his heart skipped. Nestled inside a dripping gullet was something small, rubbery. *Hideous* eyes blinked and tentacles uncoiled.

"*Kali's tit!*"

Leathery snakes punched him in the chest. Something roared as he crashed through wood and sheetrock. Everything went black.

Chapter Eight

Hiram blinked, shook his head and cursed as he struggled amid the debris in the bar's restroom. He slipped and banged his head against the wall. Another curse on his tongue, he heard something roll. He glanced up in time to see a long white cylinder pitch off a shelf above. It fell and struck his forehead.

"Piss *off!*" He grabbed the metal tube to throw it away, but large black letters caught his gaze. *INDUSTRIAL STRENGTH SANITIZER. CAUTION…*

"… aerosol contents highly flammable." Fire. *Splendid.*

Hiram glanced upwards and smiled. "Bloody hell. Maybe you don't hate me, after all."

A shrill scream came from the pub. Hiram scrambled to his feet.

Therese didn't understand what was happening, but two items were plain: that thing wanted to kill her, and the strange, *ugly* man that moved with destructive grace was the only thing stopping it—but now he was buried beneath the rubble of the restroom behind her.

The thing panted, spit wads of plasma. Its tentacles snaked back inside its belly. Flesh oozed over the horrible mass beneath. It straightened and approached her. During the fight its features had melted, but in a final cruel act, it reassumed Reggie's face and knelt before her. "*Tasty. Powerful. More than the others.*" It drooled slime.

"W-why? Why … me?"

It mimicked Reggie's voice. "*Bound to you. Must eat you. Will be fun.*" Grabbing her chin, it slammed her head against the wall. "*Reggie is still here, inside. Still wants you.*" It pinched her cheeks, forced her jaws open, and leaned forward. "*Kiss, kiss!*"

Therese's heart pounded. The Reggie-thing's mouth morphed into a cone-like snout. As it descended, she peered inside and saw a *single* large worm, nestled amongst the smaller ones, waiting for her. Something oily brushed her mind, and she screamed.

"Hello, dears. Miss me much?"

The Reggie-thing's head jerked up. Its eyes widened. Next came heat, flame, and howling.

The improvised blowtorch worked better than expected. Bluish flame engulfed the creature as it jerked away. Fire scorched its newly formed hands up to the forearms. Blackened ends smoked. A sickening odor filled the air, along with a piercing screech.

Hiram released the nozzle and shook the spray can. The Tanara'ri bounded away, crashed through *Jimmy's* front window, and fled across the narrow street into a dark alley. He followed, shaking the spray can again, realizing how foolish it was to pursue an Abyss-bound without the proper tools. For the moment, however, he had the upper hand. He meant to press it further.

Hiram followed its screams. Wind tufted refuse along the ground. Small things rustled behind rows of trash cans. Sprinting as close as he dared, he flamed away again. The glow of burning flesh lightened the alley, and the aerosol can warmed his fingertips.

He stopped. The alley had come to a dead end. What remained of the creature slumped against a brick wall, mewling. Wary of its tentacles, Hiram circled. He tried to ignore how empty the spray can felt. Once expended, he'd be weaponless. Time to end this.

He triggered the nozzle and flicked the lighter. The Tanara'ri flattened itself against the wall and screamed. Flame sputtered from the can's tip ... then nothing.

"Oh, *shit*."

The Tanara'ri leaped at him, tentacles snapping from its gut.

Tossing away the now useless spray can and lighter, Hiram dove towards the trash bins behind him. With one hand he swept a lid off one and flung it at the creature. Tentacles slapped it aside. Hiram threw up another bin cover as a battered shield. The Tanara'ri surged forward, a liquid, coiling shadow. It struck the lid, driving him back and pinning him between brick and tin. Hiram jerked and pushed. His feet scrambled in spilled trash as he fought for leverage.

A tentacle plunged for Hiram's face. He dodged, and it blasted into brick. Another tentacle glanced off his shoulder. Even as he tried to duck, more of the beast's appendages wrapped around the lid's edges, tore it from his hands and pulled him close. Hiram kicked in vain. A crude hand morphed from the swirling mass, grabbed Hiram's chin and forced his jaw open. Hiram gnashed his teeth, kicked harder, to no avail. The Tanara'ri's face elongated. It hissed and jammed its newly-formed snout between Hiram's lips. He bucked as the air in his lungs dwindled. Pulsating things filled his mouth.

Something roared, and then quickly thundered again. The Tanara'ri jerked, pulled its snout free, and howled. With a wrenching abdominal thrust, Hiram hacked up mucus and maggots. More of the things were still inside him, though, slithering down his throat.

The Tanara'ri shook its head. It lunged forward to resume its awful kiss when something *boomed* again. Hiram recognized it—the Webley. The Tanara'ri's head exploded. Bits flew as the husk dissolved. Something dark and leathery squealed and scrambled away into the trash.

Hiram sank to his knees. He felt the maggots squirming in his gut. He jammed two fingers down his throat, then vomited onto the pavement. His stomach burned, felt torn in half. He blinked through tears at his vomit. Speckled with crimson splotches, it squirmed with maggots.

He sagged onto his heels. With bleary eyes he saw his savior. Sadie? He blinked. Sadie vanished, replaced by the girl from the bar. The Webley shook in her tiny hands.

"Good show, love. Wonderful, really. Now—some help? I'm a bit winded, and I …"

The world tilted. "Oh, *damn*."

Hiram fell backward into darkness.

Therese stood still for several seconds, clenching the huge revolver. Pure adrenaline had driven her across the street. Now it faded.

Her grip relaxed. The heavy gun fell from her fingers and she fled.

Chapter Nine

Cold asphalt pressed into his back. His head ached and he drowned in nausea. He tried to roll his legs underneath him so he could stand, but they merely jerked a few times, then lay still. Seeing his Webley on the ground nearby, he pulled himself over to it and retrieved his father's weapon, clutching it uselessly in weak hands.

Hiram licked his lips and coughed. He was *tired*. So tired. *Get up, dammit. Get the hell up. Dammit, Hiram ...*

"Dammit, Hiram. Why do you *always* have to fuck things up?"

Hiram blinked. A face hovered above his. Its features shifted. One moment it was Sadie, the next his mother, then the girl from the bar ... his mysterious savior in the burning *UberNacht* ... that woman from Boston ... back to Sadie, his mother, then ...

His vision sharpened. An elvish visage hung over him, white skin gleaming, set off by midnight black hair and arched eyebrows. An eternally youthful mouth frowned.

The face disappeared. As darkness pressed down, Hiram felt delicate yet powerful hands lift and hold him close. He lost consciousness and knew no more.

PART 2

Chapter Ten

Hiram crept into his parents' bedroom. The floor creaked, and with each step a familiar dread filled him. Blood dripped from his mother's misshapen hands and bathed the smashed remains of the Guadagnini *cello at her feet. She swayed drunkenly, her back to him.*

He was an adult now, all grown up. Maybe he could stop her this time. As he got closer, however, he realized something: she didn't have Father's Webley.

His right hand grew heavy. He looked down, amazed at what he clutched: shiny, new, polished to a black sheen—the Webley as his father had always kept it. The chamber was open. Only one bullet was loaded. One for Mother.

He spun the chamber. Its clicking shattered the silence. He slapped it back into place as his heart begged, Stop this ... please! *Unheeding, he raised the Webley.*

No!

"Hiram." Several feminine voices spoke at once. "Hiram, please."

His grip tightened. The Webley shook.

His mother turned, but it wasn't her, or any one person. Its face twisted into a conglomerate mess. His mother's face twisted into Sadie's, stitched into the girl from Jimmy's. It was like a madman had hacked these women apart and patched them together into one hideous being.

"Hiram, please. You must let go."

The gun shook in his hand. Sweat poured down his face. "No. I can't. I won't."

The butchered face grimaced. "Please, Hiram. You have to. You must!*"*

"No! You can't make me!"

The thing lurched forward. "Do it! Now!"

"NO!"

It leaped for him, black eyes shining. "Then die!"

Hiram stood his ground. He did what he always did, in the end. He pulled the trigger.

Saturday Morning

"*No!*"

Hiram sat up, heart thudding. He grabbed the Webley from where it lay on the bed stand beside him and panned the room. Panic gripped him. He strained bleary eyes and aimed at imagined threats in every corner. Blinking, he tried to focus. The safe house. Empty. Nothing was disturbed, except …

He glanced at the open door before sliding from the bed, only then noticing he was shirtless. Foregoing a self-inspection, he crossed the room, limping only a bit. He ignored the slight twitch in his stomach.

Images flashed. His stomach twitched again. A voice clamored in his head, *something's in you, something's in you …*

He nudged the door wider with a foot and peered out. The hall was empty. He closed the door, locked it, and limped towards the bathroom. His mind reeled. Something wriggled in his stomach. He heard them—hissing voices—whispering in his ears and brain.

Cold, razor-edged metal slid under his Adam's apple and he froze. "Sorry for the dramatics. Wasn't sure if you'd be happy to see me. Now, be a good boy, put the gun down and have a seat."

Hiram dropped the Webley and his hands fell to his sides. He glanced down at familiar glyphs carved into the gleaming edge of the blade pressed against his neck. *I hate it when she does this.*

"Hello, Mab."

Chapter Eleven

The door stood at the end of the hall. She slipped and fell on a cold floor awash in blood. Scrambling to her feet, she ran as hard as she could. The door never got closer.

Something slithered behind her on wet skin. Shrill cries echoed, one after another. They grated against her mind. She slipped and fell again. Sweat stung her eyes as she staggered upright once more.

From the darkness, someone stepped into her path. The man from last night. There he stood, resplendent in his ridiculous suit. She raised her hands, but before she could speak, the man pulled his gun. "Sorry, love. I didn't want this. Honestly."

The giant revolver thundered.

Therese jerked awake with a cry, wrapping trembling arms around her chest. She glanced around her college flat. There were no monsters, no Reggie-thing staggered from her kitchen. There was nothing. Morning sunlight streamed through the windows. Everything was quiet.

"Reggie. Oh, *God. Reggie.*"

She covered her face with her hands and sobbed.

Chapter Twelve

Hiram reclined on the bed, smoking his pipe and sipping from a now half-empty bottle of whiskey. He took a moment to enjoy the exotic beauty perched on the windowsill. Only a moment, though. Based on her stiff posture, Mab wasn't in the mood for anything past business.

Pity.

Mab made him burn, even though he was fairly certain he hated her. She was pale-skinned, and though she possessed aristocratic features, something lewd glittered in her blue-black eyes. Like many Faerie, she looked eternally nineteen—soft but lean in all the right places. Hiram knew better. She'd lived for centuries. No one knew how the Faerie altered their appearance or achieved longevity. It wasn't magic or science. Some called them angels. To him, they were just smug assholes who thought themselves superior.

He thought how Mab must've watched Sadie die. How she must've watched him pull the trigger. Anger smoldered within. "Nice to see you again, Mab. It's been a while."

Mab shook her head like a pouting teenager. "Damn you, Hiram. You're always in the way."

He blew smoke rings towards the ceiling. "I don't know about you, love, but I'm *working*." Mab said nothing, just glared at him. For a moment, he stared back.

Those *eyes*. They belonged to the girl from *Jimmy's*.

"I don't suppose I can convince you to leave?"

"It's my job, dear. I can't just pack off with things unfinished, now can I?"

"Actually, you can. Go find some other Abyss-scum to kill.

There's plenty out there."

He sighed and set the whiskey on the floor. "Always a pleasure, Mab." His pipe now empty, he tapped its spent mix onto the carpet. "What the hell is going on?"

Her lips pursed. "Hiram … you know I can't …"

"*Bullshit!*" He jumped up and jabbed a finger into Mab's face, aware he was threatening someone who could vaporize him with a nod. He didn't care. "Don't hide behind that Faerie non-involvement shit!"

"Hiram, I …"

"No! You broke your precious code the minute you interfered and dragged me from that alley. Now, I want to know what's happening with these girls. Why were they killed? What's …"

Suddenly weary, he sat down, alarmed at the way his heart hammered and his hands shook. He rubbed his eyes. "What's going on, Mab. How are those girls connected?"

She looked away, frowning. "It's simple, really. The girl from *Jimmy's*—her name is Therese, by the way—needs to die."

"Oh, *this* should be good."

Mab tilted her head. "How much do you know about the Faerie, Hiram?"

"You mean besides their taste for bondage and their unbelievable sexual stamina? Precious little."

She gave him a harsh look, but he noticed a twinkle in her eyes. He filed that fact for later. "Besides that."

"Hell, it's all based on superstition, myth and legend." He waved. "You've been around since time began, live somewhere past the Veil. Sometimes you have visions, but they aren't completely accurate." He tapped his forehead. "Did I forget anything? Oh, right. Iron is your weakness, Kali knows why. Lastly, if the rest are like *you*, they're all hell in the sack. That's about it."

"Impressive, Hiram—really." Her smile twisted. "And actually, no,

I'm not like other Faerie at all. I'm chaste, compared to most."

"Really."

She snapped her fingers. "Focus, Hiram. What I'm about to share is sacred."

He mimed the zipping of his lips. "Stays with me, love, till death."

"Quite. In any case, your general assumptions are accurate, though we have a more rigid hierarchy than that. I'm not *just* Mab, but *Queen* Mab, and my bloodline goes back to the beginning. There've been many Mabs before me; there'll be more after. While all Faerie draw their *life force* from the Veil, the Queens have it at their fingertips. It's ours to command."

Hiram's mouth suddenly tasted dry. "Ah. *That* I didn't know." He frowned. "Wait. 'Queens.' There's more than one?"

She nodded. "Five others, six total."

"Powerful as you?"

"All equal. Balanced. That's the way it's always been. We've no idea why or how. It just is."

"Interesting. Listen, thanks for the lesson. It's been fascinating. Really. But what the hell does it have to do with five dead girls and one who'll be dead real …" He stopped and did the math. "Oh, right. Six Faerie Queens. Counting Therese, six human women. Balance." Something cold settled in his gut. "Why?"

"There must *always* be balance. Faerie Queens aren't immortal. We die of old age. Some are killed. Others step down. When that happens, the power *must* go somewhere. It must fill a new vessel."

"So these girls … they were waiting vessels for Faerie power, should a queen die?"

Mab nodded. "Theoretically, if you were fast enough or I was distracted, you could plunge an iron blade into my heart and kill me now." She eyed him. "Possible, but not probable."

"Like hell. Given the chance, I'd kick your faerie ass."

She stared at him, eyes shining. Hiram couldn't tell if she was amused, offended, or aroused. "Someday," she whispered, "I'm going to hold you to that." She composed herself and continued. "In the *unlikely* event you killed me, my power *must* go somewhere."

"Right. So in your death, the your power would go to …"

"My scion. They're Scions of the Faerie Queens."

"Nice title. Spiffy." A thought struck him. Mab and Therese's eyes. "Bloody hell. Therese is *your* scion, isn't she?"

"The latest of many."

"Many? You've had more than one?"

"Yes. Most often, we queens outlive our human scions. The Veil's power is bound inside them. They live mortal lives. In the case a scion expires, her queen must cross the Veil and bring forth another."

A sickening revelation struck him. "Mab. Is *that* what we were doing when we … all those years ago …" He swallowed. "Did you use me to sire a scion?"

Mab snorted. "Hiram, please! With you I had a scratch and itched it. That's all." She leered at him. "And scratched it well, you did, I might add … for a human."

"*Focus*, Mab."

She chuckled and flicked her ponytail. "Right. To birth a scion, a queen must cross over, choose a mate, assume the trappings of everyday human life—which doesn't include bondage dens in Texas, I'm afraid."

"I thought it was Montana."

"Like you'd remember. Of course, the relationships are always whirlwind romances. There's more time to replace a scion than a queen, but we don't have forever."

"You enchant the poor dupes? How utterly unsurprising."

Mab's face grew serious. "Actually, no. For whatever reason, the scions must be born of something like true love."

"Ah. That's why you and I couldn't have …"

Mab rushed on, but he felt sure her eyes flickered. "And then, of course, because queens can't very well stay and raise a family, the unit is eventually dissolved."

"Yes. All those orphan girls." His jaw clenched. "Lots of broken families to produce an heir."

"Collateral damage. Worth keeping balance. Besides," something entirely different flashed in her eyes, "we've all been through it. Scions ascend, change … and after that, their previous mortal lives don't matter anymore." Somehow, Hiram suspected she wasn't being entirely truthful. On this point, however, he kept his peace.

She continued. "In any case, uncalled scions grow up to be isolated women living solitary lives. They remain mortal, though their lives do shimmer with a dim reflection of the Veil's beauty."

Hiram thought hard. "I see the crisis. Someone was either foolish enough—or *powerful* enough—to summon the Tanara'ri to eliminate your bench, so you can't call up reserves when needed." He frowned. "A crude analogy, but it fits."

"Yes. It's alarming that someone discovered the scions at all." Her eyes flashed. "No one is supposed to know they exist, *plus* they're protected. No one should be able to work a locator spell on them, much less bind something to them."

"How are they protected?"

Mab fingered beneath the neck of her tunic, withdrawing a chain from which dangled a small charm. Hiram narrowed his eyes and inspected it. The charm looked simple; a silver circle split down the middle with a lightning bolt, an engraved book and quill on one side, three small crystals embedded on the other.

"Every child is left with a small charm like this. They're specific to each queen's line; *this* charm is the Sigil of Mab. They're wards that cloak the Veil power bound within the scions. It's not working now because all the power that's flowed into Therese is too much for it to cloak. That still begs the question as to why it didn't work with the other scions."

"Interesting. According to Bothwell, all the dead girls apparently received medallions that were sigils of the Tanara'ri. Focusing agents, I imagine. Probably strong enough to break the wards."

"That still doesn't explain how someone knew who they were so the medallions could be sent to them."

"No, it doesn't. I wonder, though …"

"What?"

Hiram leaned forward. "Well, it's strange. Why all the girls one night, then Therese the next? Something either broke the Binding pattern and it had to reset itself, or …" He shook his head. He'd come back to it later.

"As disturbing as that is, there are other, greater concerns."

Hiram looked up too quickly, and his stomach surged. He swallowed, fought back a wave of nausea, and said, "I imagine this is where you try to convince me that Therese needs to die, though I've got an inkling, now. It's all about balance, isn't it?"

Mab hugged herself, looking ever more like an anxious teenager. "Yes. Just as there must be balance among the queens, there must be balance among the scions. Normally, the situation isn't so dire. There's usually plenty of time to birth another scion or two."

"But you've never had this many missing scions before, this much loose energy."

"No."

"So too much power has been displaced, and there's not enough time to … birth … replacement scions, correct?"

"Worse. Because of its sheer volume, the power has flowed into the only remaining vessel that can contain it: Therese."

"What happens if Therese dies?"

Mab glanced away. "Without a vessel to attract it, the power will remain trapped in the ether, safe ... until a new cycle of scions can be started. However, the power now within Therese will soon reach critical mass. When it does, it'll break her binding. She'll manifest. Indeed, she's probably already manifested in small ways."

"What will happen to her?"

"She won't be human, but she won't ascend, either. She'll become ... something else."

"So what's the problem? I can sense evil, Mab ... I know what darkness is like; you of all people know that. She looked like a pretty generic kid. Even if she manifests fully, I can't imagine she'd become evil."

She looked back at him and raised an eyebrow. "You don't have to be evil to be dangerous. Besides, humans weren't meant to hold that kind of power. I know you think us smug, but the Faerie have been bred for this." She gave him an arch look. "The Veil's power consumes and overwhelms. Given your mother's fate, *you* of all people should know *that*."

His stomach twisted, but before he could respond, Mab continued. "I've had a vision, Hiram. Seen what's to come."

"Oh, well—excuse me. We know how accurate *those* are."

She looked at him with an odd glint in her eye. "Would you care to see?"

Hiram sighed. "Well, there's no way I'm going along with this on your word alone ..."

Mab cut him off and grabbed his wrist, fingernails digging into his skin. Her touch burned. His eyes rolled back as the Veil flowed into him.

"See then, Hiram Grange. See ... and *understand*."

Chapter Thirteen

Hiram thrashed. A rushing sound filled his ears. Everything else faded as darkness fell.

"See, Hiram Grange. See what I've seen, and tremble at the sight."

Something exploded in the distance, then he *saw*—the land laid to waste, ground burning with white flame. Buildings burnt to ashes. Rubble piled high amid swirling rivers of white fire. The liquid flame surged everywhere.

In the distance, he saw them: Three figures suspended in the air. The sky around them churned with the same white fire. *Things* circled them, fantastic terrors that snapped and clawed and ripped at each other. They where shifting things of leathery hide, with blackened eyes and glass talons. He knew what they were, and where they'd come from: the Abyss.

He looked back to the three floating figures. One hovered in front, the remaining two flanked. The central figure burned with the Veil. It all came from *her*, and he knew: she'd torn down the barriers between the Abyss and the Earth.

Shadows concealed the figure on the left. The other, however, he realized in cold fear … *was him*. Crackling with white fire.

Far away over the hills, thunder rolled. He caught a glimpse of something white and hungry. When he looked back at the horrible floating trinity, he saw the most terrifying thing of all: Therese, *laughing*, over and over …

Mab withdrew her hand. Hiram tumbled but she caught him with one arm. His stomach clenched, he coughed, and *things* wriggled inside him as Mab eased him back down onto the bed. He was so stricken by the vision; he didn't have the strength to feel embarrassed.

"Thanks for that, Mab—really. As if I didn't have enough nightmares rattling around in my head. What's one more?"

She didn't seem concerned. "I'm sorry, but you wanted to see." She settled back onto the windowsill. "Do you understand now?"

Hiram nodded. The image of Therese and the man at her side. "Yes. That was me in the vision, wasn't it? Next to Therese."

"It was."

Hiram shook his head. "So in other words, if Therese doesn't die before her power manifests, not only will she destroy the world, but I'll join her. Thanks for the trust."

"Still having sweet dreams of Sadie? Still willing to do *anything* to bring her back?"

His jaw tightened. Not for the first time, he wished an iron blade near to hand. "How the hell do you …?"

"Don't dissemble. You're *broken*, Hiram Grange—even more so than usual because of what you did to Sadie. What would you become if offered the Veil's power, and could fulfill your every desire?"

A chill crept up his spine as he looked away. "A monster."

She sighed, sounding oddly regretful. "The cruel fact is this: If you walk away now … as terrible as this sounds … Therese will be killed before she manifests. The Tanara'ri will consume her, end the Binding. Regrettable, yes. However, the power of the Scions will return to the ether, the cycle can begin anew, and disaster will be averted."

He raised an eyebrow. "Excluding everyone who dies before that."

"I'm thinking large scale."

"Of course. Silly me."

"However, if you're *not* going to walk away, you must destroy the vessel. After last night, she'll trust you. Destroy the vessel, Hiram. Loose the power of the Veil."

"Look, I'm no saint—hell, I'm not even a good person—but that's monstrous. Walking away and letting those things kill her is terrible. But to wheedle my way close, gain her trust, then murder her?"

Mab's face hardened into a regal mask. "You've seen what's to come."

Hiram leaned forward, his neck tight with anger. "I also know that your visions can be wrong, or interpreted differently. You're not omnipotent."

"This isn't a pissing contest. It's bigger than you and me. It may sound cold, but because you saved her, she's now a danger to us all."

"Let me get this straight. After figuring all this out, you're content to let the girl die, simply because it'd make things more convenient for you?"

"This *isn't* about convenience …"

Someone knocked on the door, interrupting her. "*Mr. Robertson? Mr. Freddy Robertson? Package, sir.*"

Damn. He shook his head. A courier *would* come now. Just his luck. To Mab he said, "Of course it is. When it comes to the Faerie, it's always about their convenience."

"*Mr. Robertson?*" Another knock. Mab ignored it, continued to stare at him with her haunting eyes.

He affected a yawn. "You know, this has been great, but I've got work to do. Got to see a girl about destroying the world. As always, it's been fabulous gabbing, but you need to be off."

"*Mr. Freddy Robertson?*"

"Hold on! I'm coming!" He stood, but Mab moved and blocked his path with her shoulder, pushing back with surprising strength.

"What are you going to do?"

An intriguing truth struck him. "Well, I'll be damned. You're *afraid* ... aren't you?"

Resentment burned off her. "*What* are you going to do?"

Her frustration emboldened him. "Here's the thing, Mab. I don't trust you, or the Faerie. Until this moment, you've largely left the Tanara'ri and their Summoner out of this. Why is that, I wonder?"

"Are you suggesting that we'd bind these things to our own scions? That I'd help destroy balance?"

"*Mr. Robertson?*"

"A moment! I'm naked! With schoolgirls! Lots of them!" Turning to Mab, he scowled. "I've no idea, but you're not human, are you? I couldn't begin to guess your motivations. Either way, I'll keep my own counsel."

"*I have a package for Mr. Robertson.*"

"Sweet Kali's tit!" Shaking his head, he continued. "Now, if you'll excuse me, I've got things to do: monsters to hunt, a talisman to find, a girl to save, and a fucking peon at the door who obviously can't tell I'm busy. In the interim, your prophecy can go to hell."

He shoved her aside, even though he knew she could throw him through the window if she chose. All traces of emotion drained from Mab's voice as she intoned, "So you're willing to doom all humanity to destruction, then?"

"*Mr. Robertson ...*"

He gave her a crooked, humorless smile as he grasped the doorknob. "At least I'm human, Mab. That gives me more say than you'll ever have."

"*... package, sir.*"

His patience breached, he jerked open the door. "Hell and damnation, what's *wrong* with you? Are you deaf, or just bleedin' ..."

Standing to one side was a tall, thin man bearing an eerie resemblance to himself. Dressed in a charcoal-black suit of similar though more modern cut, he stood rigid, hands clasped before him. Thin lips pressed together and ice-cold blue eyes blazed at Hiram from under cropped blond-white hair.

The loathed Alphonse Kline the Third, but that meant …

He looked next to Kline, and down. Dressed in a prim, neat gray business suit was a walking portrait of everyone's favorite grandmother, mound of gray curls and all. Mrs. Bothwell peered at Hiram quizzically through ornate glasses.

"Mr. Robertson. I do hope we're not intruding."

Chapter Fourteen

Therese stood in her living room. Sunlight streamed through the only open window. Dust and other particles hung suspended in the beam, paying silent witness to her wonderment and horror. It was her painting—the one shoved in the corner. Staring at it, clutching the dusty drop cloth that had covered the thing, she knew with lingering sadness it was a masterpiece no one would ever see. That's why she'd been unable to get rid of it, horrible as it was.

Before last night, it had been easy to dismiss the painting and its implications, shoved in a corner, shrouded by an old cloth. Before last night, it had also been easy to dismiss her dreams as pure fancy and nothing more.

Everything had changed. After retrieving the man's gun, she'd pulled the trigger with little thought. Somehow, despite her shaking arms and the weight of the weapon, she'd managed to hurt the ... *thing* ... that looked like Reggie. In the cool reason of daylight, it was amazing she'd hit anything at all, or hadn't accidentally shot the man instead. No, she'd shot true, as if an extra sense had guided her. She didn't even remember pulling the trigger. All she recalled was the strange certainty that she'd hit the target. And she had. She'd shot the thing's head, and it had exploded.

She remembered the man throwing up, thanking her, then passing out. The *right* thing would've been to help him, but she hadn't done that. She'd dropped the gun. Ran. Her next memory was at a phone booth, miles down the street, blubbering for a cab. Somehow, she made it back home in one piece, where she'd collapsed into bed.

She'd no explanations for last night. In a fit of denial, she'd called Reggie's cell phone several times after waking, but it was out of service. She then called his work, but they'd received no calls either.

Reggie was dead. Something had killed him, taken his shape, even his voice. Then, for reasons unknown to her, it had tried to kill her. So here she was, staring at that awful yet beautiful painting, the morning after the most horrifying night of her life. Where did she go from here?

She gripped the drop cloth tightly. She'd always known she was different from everyone else, and not just because she was an orphan. Not because of her painting, either. Painting had been the medium she'd fallen in love with. She could've chosen anything: writing, music, chalk, clay. Her true talents lay not in her art, but inside her.

There was no going back. She was different. Always had been. Last night something had wanted to kill her. A man stopped it. An ugly, almost repulsive man to be sure, but a man who moved with a deadly grace, nonetheless.

According to the painting, he couldn't stop it forever. Maybe he was even the cause. Deep inside—in that way people sometimes have—she knew if she saw him again … he'd kill her.

Hating it, but not knowing what else to do, Therese moved to pack her things for the only recourse left to her.

Running.

Chapter Fifteen

"For heaven's sake, Hiram. Come sit down."

Fully dressed, Hiram stood at the window, hands clasped behind his back, shoulders tensed. Few people shamed him. One was Mrs. Bothwell; the second Punjabi, the old spiritualist cook at Delacore Academy who had raised him after Mother committed suicide. The third, of course, had been Father, who he'd neither seen nor heard from since his disappearance, so it hardly mattered.

Bothwell was his handler at the ambiguous Office of Investigative Research and Analysis. She sent him out into the field to locate and destroy the varied beings that snuck out through confluences, earthbound doorways from the Abyss. And while her prim, fastidious demeanor may be viewed by most as the affectations of a gentle woman, he knew the truth. Though she tolerated his quirks, even cleaned up such messes as the *Jodie Incident*, and provided for his specific ... needs, Bothwell's no-nonsense attitude when it came to Work and his assignments was resolute. The hard glint in her eyes never seemed to falter, no matter the amount of blood spilled—whether that of an Abyssal-spawn or even Hiram's.

Mrs. Bothwell sighed. "Please, Hiram—*sit*. I'm not here to reprimand you. We've far too much to do." Hiram glanced over his shoulder. Mrs. Bothwell smiled and gestured at the chair across from her. "Please."

He nodded and flexed his shoulders, loosening stiff muscles. Feeling as if he were back in Headmaster Weil's office at Delacore, Hiram walked to the chair across from Bothwell and sat down. Thankfully, the loathsome Kline had departed after leaving a black oblong suitcase and a canvas satchel larger than his personal bag.

Mab, of course, had vanished. Bothwell appeared to believe his story, but he hadn't missed Kline's amused, cryptic smile. Damned lackey, anyway.

Mrs. Bothwell removed her glasses from her nose and polished them with great care, using a handkerchief from her handbag. "I have to admit, I'm not sure what to say. Only five hours here and you identify the next target, then acquit yourself well with minimal data and without the proper tools." Finished with her polishing, she replaced her glasses and favored him with a gaze of admiration, mixed with consternation. "I don't know whether to be proud or annoyed."

"Mrs. Bothwell, I …"

She held up a firm yet gentle hand. "As I said, we haven't the time for our customary banter. This assignment requires an unusual amount of expediency."

"Expediency and your personal presence on site. I haven't seen you in the field since that mess in Argentina."

"Indeed, but as I said, this case has developed disturbing new facets that require much closer supervision."

"Yes. This girl Therese, Mab's involvement … among other things."

A short, businesslike nod, so ill-fitting of her grandmotherly appearance. "Yes, and five other dead girls."

He nodded and was about to speak, when a tickle in his throat interrupted him. He coughed and massaged his chest.

Mrs. Bothwell frowned. "Hiram, are you all right?"

"Quite. Chest cold." *Liar.*

Mrs. Bothwell pursed her lips. "In any case, Mab's story seems consistent with our background checks. All the victims were orphans. Some grew up in institutions, others bounced between foster homes." She paused. "All had connections to the arts. A musician, a sculptor, a dancer, a fortune teller, even; and the last, Allison McTavey, a freshman at Ulster University's College of Art & Design."

"And then Therese. Interesting."

"Of course, Faerie involvement complicates matters."

"Yes, it does—arrogant, smug bastards."

"Nevertheless; we've work to do. Someone wanted these girls dead and summoned the Tanara'ri for the job."

"That makes more sense now. Calling something like that to kill humans seemed like overkill."

Bothwell nodded. "I agree. Our primary objective is still to find the talisman or conduit. I've gained you access to the underground maintenance tunnels in University Quarter. You're to meet a man named Stemmins; he's the university vice-provost. He's to conduct you to the History and Archeology Department's artifact room to search for 'fraudulent artifacts.' Get out from underneath him any way you can, but take care and be wary. He's a prickly, suspicious fellow. Bit of an ass, I'm afraid."

Hiram licked his lips and smiled. He knew he shouldn't, but he couldn't resist. "I detect an air of bitterness, Mrs. Bothwell. An old beau, perhaps?"

A sniff of disdain. "Hardly my type. At all. The man lacks sexual stamina."

"Well." Hiram swallowed and tried not to make a face. "*That* certainly gave me several images I'd rather not have, so onward to other things, yes? What about Therese?"

"Hopefully you'll encounter her again. For now, containment first as always."

Hiram nodded. "So—you've got something that'll work against these things?"

Bothwell grinned. "Oh, yes. Something unique that should dispatch them nicely." She paused, then added, "The device is experimental, which I know you despise, but the manufacturer's reputation is unparalleled."

"As always, I'll make do." He stood, walked to the dresser bureau and opened the case left by Kline. He couldn't help but whistle at the short-barreled shotgun inside. "Smashing." Though he preferred his precious Webley, this new weapon should help. He lifted the gun out and caressed its sleek, destructive lines while Bothwell recited its specifications.

"It's a one-of-a-kind semi-automatic Franchi, based on the SPAS-15, top of the line. Because the ammunition has been designed specially, a modified six-round box magazine has been developed instead of the customary eight-round."

Hiram frowned and peered down the gun's breech. Specially designed ammunition was often a capricious bedfellow, prone to misfiring. "Specially designed? How so?"

"Are you familiar with 'Dragon's Breath'?"

"Ammunition developed in the seventies. Outlawed because the cartridges used an exothermic, pyrophoric metal too unstable for practical use."

"Yes. A special brand of Zirconium was used for *these* shell casings. More stable. Generates a sizable burst of elemental flame with each shot."

"Fabulous. What else?"

"The slug itself is made of Orichalium."

Hiram almost smiled. "Quite. The infamous space metal that transformed a tribe of aboriginal humans into the first Illuminati. According to legend, anyway."

Mrs. Bothwell appeared at his elbow and nodded. "Yes. Now, no one has ever actually *seen* Orichalium in nature. Ours was synthetically made. However, it contains all the storied ingredients."

"And those are?"

"According to our texts, trace elements of copper, gold, silver, and iron. The iron isn't concentrated enough to dispatch faeries." She paused, smiled at him. "When we detected the quantum fluctuations, however, I took the liberty of having several boxes of iron bullets made for the Webley."

Hiram thought again of Mab and her smugness. "Excellent."

She tapped the satchel Kline had left. "As usual, we've also provided you with magnesium flares; necrotic tissue being allergic to them, of course." She offered him an apologetic glance. "I'm sorry we didn't have them waiting last night. A little problem with slipping through customs, because of something extra we've provided."

"Oh?"

"We've given you a small store of plastic explosives, C-4 to be exact, along with infrared detonators." She raised an eyebrow. "I only expect them to be used in the direst of circumstances. I'm still receiving bills from your *last* adventure with C-4."

"Oh, please. Those city officials were complete asses about that. I *got* the goblins, didn't I? Wiped out a whole nest, if I remember."

"Yes, but you also incinerated an entire elementary school."

Hiram snorted. "Hell's bells. It was holiday, the place was empty, and don't tell me those kids weren't absolutely *thrilled* to miss more school." He paused and then amended, "Even if they did lose a hamster or two."

"Indeed. In any case, please be more judicious this time, will you?"

Hiram grabbed a magazine and slapped it home. With a vigorous thrust, he pumped the shotgun, loading a round in the chamber with a satisfying *cha-chuk*, and rested the barrel on his shoulder. He favored Bothwell with a manic grin. "Of course. Judicious is my middle name."

PART 3

Chapter Sixteen

University Quarter, Underground Access Tunnels

Their mingled footsteps bounced off concrete walls, echoing back upon them throughout the subterranean space. "This is a waste of my time. I've many, many more important things I could be doing."

Vice-provost Stemmins was proving to be an asshole, indeed. "I'm sorry for the inconvenience," Hiram squawked in a peevish voice, cultivated for his role, "but the International Consortium of Universities takes grant fraud very seriously." He pursed his lips, tried to appear mousy, and did his best not to picture Bothwell *with* this man … or with any man, for that matter. "This year alone, thousands in funds have been wasted on forgeries, which has prompted us to audit *all* the universities under our umbrella." Hiram played his cover story to a tee, as he'd had years of practice in perfecting his role as an auditor for the non-existent agency.

"I've never even *heard* of this so-called Consortium. I've a mind to call the Grant Funding Bureau for your credentials."

"You're welcome to. However, I still need your records." Luckily, Bothwell had several well-paid moles working at the Bureau. Any snoopers would find nothing but solid credentials.

Stemmins grunted. "What do you need again?"

"I need to verify that all forms have proper signatures and that they match precisely the items in your collection."

Stemmins gestured at the Franchi's case, which Hiram carried in his right hand. "What's that? Large case for paperwork."

"This? Standard carbon dating tools."

"Carbon dating?"

"Yes. To test suspect items for authenticity."

The man stiffened. "Really."

"Rest assured. Should I find any forgeries, if your paperwork is in order; we'll exact justice *for* you, not against."

Stemmins flashed an unconvincing smile over his shoulder. "How reassuring."

"We do our best."

A tight nod. "This way."

Hiram swallowed and shoved down a cold, twisting nausea in his gut. The things inside him writhed as he fell in behind the vice-provost.

Therese shifted from one foot to the other, resettling the backpack on her shoulders for what seemed like the hundredth time. Packing had been quick, really. She'd grabbed enough clothes for several days, along with all the cash and snacks she could scrounge, then dashed to the University Quarter's main bus terminal. Because she lived on the edge of campus, that had taken longer than she'd wanted. However, she'd made it before the next scheduled wave of buses left … only to get stuck in a line that defied explanation.

It allowed her to think about things more than she wanted.

She shifted again, blew stray hair from her eyes. Ridiculous, really. The line hadn't moved since she'd gotten here. It was almost as if no one manned the terminal, and everyone in line only pretended to wait …

A light touch caressed her thoughts. Whispering. Talking. *Buzzing*.

A thin, blond girl two persons ahead shuffled around, arms hanging slack, mouth open as she stared. A young man in front of the blond also turned and stared.

An alarm jangled in Therese's head. On shaking legs she backed away and looked around. Everyone in the bus terminal stared at her. She wanted to scream, but her breath caught in her throat when she heard a soft, fleshy ripping. As her gaze shivered around the room, stomachs split open, exposing tentacles and gleaming eyes.

"*Hello, Therese. Good to see you again.*"

Therese gasped. The *things* parted to allow *Its* approach. Her heart jackhammered.

"N-no … no, no, no, no …" Her hand dug into her pocket for something sharp.

The Reggie-thing approached, its face scarred and twisted from the gunshot in the alley. Tentacles uncoiled from its torn belly. Nestling eyes glared at her. "Hello, Therese. Give us a kiss, will you?"

In her pocket, she found her keys. Slowly, she pulled them free.

It leaned in, reptilian tongue tasting the air. Unable to take any more, Therese screamed and jammed her keys into one of the Reggie-thing's bloated eyes. Fluid spurted. The ruined eyeball melted, running down the stolen face.

It laughed.

Chapter Seventeen

Hiram set down the Franchi's case and assessed the archival room. Statues, totems, even stone peace pipes lined the tables in rows. Masks and ancient diadems hung on the walls. "Impressive." He walked down the middle aisle, shifted his satchel and rummaged inside.

"Quite. What now? I hate to be redundant, but I've work to do."

"I don't want to keep you." Hiram withdrew the small, hand-held electromagnetic scanner. "I'm going to check these items against a digital manifest that lists suspected forgeries sold on the market within the past ten years."

"You're going to check *every* item?"

"We consider ourselves very thorough, Mr. Stemmins."

"What the hell am I supposed to do until you finish?"

Hiram nodded towards the door. "Please bring me your authorized purchase orders. It would speed up the process."

"Fine. Don't touch anything until I return."

"Wouldn't think of it." There was no answer, however, save that of a door opening and closing. Hiram turned his full attention to the scanner. He didn't like using technology. Like magic, it felt like a cheat. In this instance, however, he didn't have a choice.

He activated the scanner. A yellow bar appeared on the device's small screen. He'd calibrated it for the room's perimeter. Anything used to conjure a confluence would be highly charged with residual electromagnetic energies. Of course, a talisman needn't be an object in this room. It could be any object that had absorbed residual confluent energy from a supernaturally turbulent event. A *Slushie* cup dropped by a student at the Columbine massacre or even a rabbit's foot found at Chernobyl would work.

Worst case, the conduit would be a person. He'd certainly *eliminated* plenty of those. This was the best place to start, however. Perhaps, for once, he'd stumble across fortune and the conduit *would* be an object, and not another human life he'd have to snuff out, so soon after …

Sadie.

He shook his head. Containment first. Find the talisman, destroy the binding, banish the Tanara'ri. If the girl survived that long, he'd rescue her, too—the universe and Mab be buggered.

He coughed wetly, lungs aching. He massaged his chest and realized a cold truth: by the time this ended, he could be dead. The least he could do was kill some more monsters, save an innocent girl, and put a notch in the 'win' column before he took the last, big ride.

Chapter Eighteen

The EM scanner emitted an increasingly high-pitched screech as the yellow bar shaded to red. He adjusted the settings as he passed the last table. It whined higher. The back wall, then.

He waved the scanner over mounted artifacts. Moving outward in widening circles, the whine decreased in pitch. Reversing his direction, he slowly spiraled inward. The pitch rose as the yellow bar once again deepened to crimson. Three sweeps later the scanner produced a piercing whine over a tarnished bronze chalice, hung near shoulder height. The indicator burned bright red.

"Excellent." He deactivated the scanner and stowed it in his pocket. "Let's end this, then." He reached for the chalice.

The instant his fingertips brushed metal, pain seized his hand and flashed down his arm, vibrating his muscles to the bone. Howling, he grabbed his wrist and pulled. No good. The pain only increased. Numbness crept through his burning fingers. If he didn't do something soon, he'd lose his hand, perhaps even his arm.

"Eteru, *palasu*."

Hiram's hand jerked free. He stumbled and almost fell. Arcs of pain shot all the way to his shoulder.

"Kali's *tit!* I *hate* magic!"

"Not a very enlightened perspective, really."

Hiram straightened and flexed his aching hand. Tendrils of smoke wafted from his blackened fingers. He glared at Vice-Provost Stemmins, who stood inside the doorway, hands in his pockets, smiling.

"I can empathize with your consternation, though. Nasty little ward, that. If I'd let the magic run its course, the nerves in your arm would've been fried. You'd do well to thank me."

He shook his stinging hand. "Well, I was going to shoot your ass, but I suppose my thanks will have to do."

"You're not really from some Consortium, are you? And you're not here about grant fraud."

Hiram faced Stemmins and adjusted his jacket in a vain attempt to restore some dignity. "Actually, that depends on what you conjured with that chalice."

"I don't suppose money will help this go away?"

"What? People are *dead*. Dammit, man, *I* might die, which is far worse. No, I don't suppose money will do." Hiram thought for a moment, then added, "Well, it'd take more than you have, anyway."

Stemmins frowned. "Deaths? What deaths?" Before Hiram could answer, Stemmins waved him off. "No one has died. Some have possibly suffered moderate degradation along the way ... but that's all."

"What the *hell* are you talking about?"

"You recognize the chalice?"

Hiram glanced over his shoulder and studied it. "Looks like a remnant of the Assyrian Empire, or perhaps late Persia."

"Quite astute. Its previous owner was the Marquis de Sade."

"*Oh*." Hiram glanced at Stemmins, impressed in spite of himself.

"Yes. If you know about the Marquis' final days, you'll understand my ... affection for this piece."

Hiram thought quickly. "Right. He immersed himself in the dark arts and ... bloody hell. You're using the damn thing to conjure a succubus, aren't you? Maybe even involving a few students as well?"

Stemmins smiled an edged rictus. "Perhaps. However, I assure you no one has died. Yet."

"Son of a bitch. Two confluences in the same place?" Hiram scowled at the man. "Why does this shit always happen to *me*?"

"I've no idea what you're talking about. No matter." Smoothly, Stemmins drew a nickel-plated Walther PPK from his pocket, thumbed the safety off, and pointed it at Hiram.

Hiram's spine froze as a ludicrous situation shifted to a deadly one. "Hold on. If all you've done is conjured hell-whores for some demonic shagging, I've got no quarrel with you." He calculated how quickly he could draw the Webley and didn't like the odds. "There are much *bigger* things going on here."

"Honestly—I don't care."

"What? Why the hell not?"

Stemmins shrugged but kept the gun trained on Hiram. "Because I've done things no one can know about. Blasted Catholics and Protestants are a bit persnickety about black magic and decadence, you see. Wouldn't put me in a very good light, now would it? And, ironically, I *did* misuse a research grant to purchase the chalice." He shrugged. "You see the job-related implications. I'd be sacked. Ruined."

"Honestly, man, I haven't the time for …"

His insides quivered. Behind Stemmins, several shadows filled the doorway. A low buzzing assaulted his mind; an oily feeling of dread, loathing, and naked hunger brushed his spirit.

FEED!

Hiram's knees buckled. His head pounded and stomach churned. The creatures in the doorway had partly gestated. Slimy masses with pulsating eyes nestled in their distended abdomens. Maggot-riddled faces leered as they lurched forward.

Stemmins frowned. "What the hell is wrong with you?"

No longer worried about Stemmins, Hiram backed up, digging into his satchel while *They* pressed against his mind.

FEED!

The beasts crept into the room. Thousands of voices screamed in his head. He'd suffered psychic attacks before, but this was different. It melded with him until he couldn't tell where he ended and it began, and his mind burned under their gazes …

Chapter Nineteen

Therese shook as they surrounded her. Their oily skin leaked awful fluids, and they stared with empty eyes. Rivers of maggots squirmed from their slack-jawed mouths. Their bellies curdled as *things* pushed against thin skin. Others had great holes torn in them, from which tentacles flailed. Something in the dripping hollows of their guts blinked hungry eyes.

And Reggie ... poor, insecure Reggie ... stood before her, maggot-ridden face oozing. Viscous fluids trickled from the eye she'd stabbed. Patches in his hair exposed raw swaths of red meat. His belly had split open, revealing the thing inside. Serpentine tentacles coiled around his body and reached for her.

The Reggie-thing laughed as *It* plucked the keys from the ruined eye, tipped *Its* head back, and swallowed them. Smacking pus-slick lips, *It* buzzed, "*Not nice, Therese. Not nice at all.*"

The horrible voice clanged against her ears, and a primal, liquid fear slithered in her thighs. This thing that wore Reggie's face was simply not right. She tried to speak, scream ... but she wilted inside.

"*Shhh. It's all right, Therese. You'll understand everything when you're part of the Hive.*" A bloated finger caressed her cheek, left behind a thin trail of slime that crawled on her skin, felt alive. "*You'll know everything, because you'll be one with us ... forever.*"

The coiled thing in *Its* belly shifted, expelling rank odors, making her gag. She closed her eyes, so she wouldn't have to see it when they took her.

"N-no, no, no, no, *no* ..."

"*Poor Therese. We'll make it easier. We'll allow Reggie back up for a bit.*"

Silence. Something shifted. Then the being spoke in such an eerie imitation of Reggie, she was almost convinced that if she opened her eyes, he'd be there.

"*Hey love. Sorry for this.*" *It* paused. Therese sobbed and bit her lip. Something squelched and slid. She imagined the slit in his stomach widening as tentacles billowed out to envelop her. Something leathery coiled down her leg, wrapped around her thigh, knee, curled at her ankle. She gasped as something wet clasped her hands.

"*I never treated you right, Therese; never really deserved you. I see that now.*"

Bits of her soul tore away. Therese shuddered, weak with exhaustion, fear, hopelessness. The darkness behind her closed eyes spared her the horrible sight of this *thing* wrapping around her, but also tortured her because she wanted to believe that *Reggie* held her close, and not this monster.

"*There, there. It's all right. No more tears. The Hive has shown me wonderful things. In a moment, you'll see. Then we can be together, like we were meant to be.*"

Something licked her face and swabbed the tears off her cheeks. A buzzing choir of thousands pierced her mind with one refrain: *EAT YOU, EAT YOU, EAT YOU…*

Something inside her snapped. A wall tumbled down and released what had been growing there: Rage.

She hated this *thing* that dared appear as the man she might've loved. She hated how *It* invaded her mind, pushed into her dark places. She hated them all. She wanted them to *burn*.

Her body tingled. From a well deep inside, a white, blazing river flowed. She mounted it, rode its waves.

She opened her eyes. Everything glowed in shades of bluish white… except *them*. They pulsed, black splotches of death and decay.

They needed to be *cleansed*.

Chapter Twenty

The artifact room shuddered, throwing Hiram and Stemmins to the floor. Across the room, the Tanara'ri shrieked and collapsed. Hiram rolled onto his stomach, blazing with newfound resolve as the pressure against his mind faded. He still felt weakened from the things inside him, but for the moment, his mind was free.

Tentacles thumped against the ground and beat out weird, staccato rhythms as the creatures wailed. Something had hurt them. "Therese." He stood.

The beasts howled again. Stemmins rolled over and screamed like a teenage girl. Maybe even worse than the girls he'd ministered to in this very room. Poetic, really.

From his satchel, Hiram plucked two magnesium flares. A Tanara'ri flipped to its humanoid feet and howled in a language that burned against his brain. Its humanoid face morphed into a low-slung maw. Clusters of malevolent red eyes blinked in its twisting belly.

"Holy ... *SHITE!* Grange, what the hell is that?"

Hiram strode past the man. "That, Stemmins, is what I meant by 'bigger things going on.'" With his teeth, he ripped the plastic end caps off the flares and they burst into silvery-white nimbi of fire. Hiram's lips and cheeks burned where glowing embers landed.

The beasts screamed again. And of course, *past* them was the Franchi.

"D-did I do this?"

"No! They're the reason I'm here, not your precious little demon sluts. They would've been *much* easier to deal with, however! More fun, too!"

The lead Tanara'ri lumbered forward, screeching. To his disgust, the things inside him twitched, yearning to be connected to their Hive. Something oily brushed his mind. Hiram's teeth ground as psychic fingers pried deep into his thoughts.

EAT YOU EAT YOU EAT YOU EAT YOU!

Hiram swept the flares low and focused on his goal: the Franchi. There were too many of the things for his Webley to be useful for long. He needed the wide fire of the shotgun's special slugs.

"On second thought, this might also be fun." Hiram readied himself for a charge.

The Tanara'ri roared. Stemmins screamed. Hiram bellowed.

The beasts flung themselves forward.

Blue fire. Pulsing in waves from her, touching everything, purifying, burning away blackness.

<Burn it down.>

W-what is this?

<You are the one, Therese ... The Chosen One. All the scions are dead, save you—the last vessel. All will tremble, all will rejoice, all will serve.>

<All will be cleansed.>

What's happening to me?

<Darkness must be destroyed.>

I ... I don't understand! Please!

<Burn it down, Therese. Burn the world, rid it of darkness, leave it pure ... and empty.>

No!

The power faded, and the white river receded into its well. She still sensed it there: a silvery, glowing pinprick, trapped behind a wall once more. It had left a tendril behind. For now, it lay inert.

Therese came back to herself as sputtering droplets of water fell on her brow. They multiplied into a downpour. Therese shivered, soaked. She felt cold ... but she *lived*.

She opened her eyes and gasped at the destruction before her.

The room was scorched, piled ash sludging under the emergency sprinklers. The tables and chairs in the terminal waiting area were twisted, melted beyond recognition into burnt metal and charred plastic. Everything sizzled and popped and hissed. Steam rose in swirling columns. Here and there, small fires flickered and died. The air shimmered with the lingering heat of her destruction.

Her destruction. From her hands. *She'd* done this, destroyed everything. A hollow pit opened in her stomach as she recalled the merciless voice in her head. *Burn it down.* She looked around again. The monsters had been destroyed, all of them except ...

Frowning, she peered through the watery streams. She felt a low buzz at the edge of her mind, and her guts clenched. Something flailed at the room's edge. Leathery tentacles slapped wet concrete. A high-pitched keening split the air, drowning out the distant fire alarms.

And then ... the buzzing filled her mind. There, pushing itself upright, was one of *them*: fully grown, at last. Its hide glistened in the artificial rain and tentacles slithered in the disintegrating mass of its destroyed husk. It screamed and lurched towards her.

Therese felt the white river flicker. She closed her eyes and reached for it, found the tendril it had left. She tugged, tried to pull down the wall, release the fire. She felt a glimmering of power, a tingling in her fingers ... then nothing.

She opened her eyes as the thing shrieked again. It had halved the distance between them.

"Shite!"

She turned and fled. The Tanara'ri thrashed after her. She had one chance, and it loomed before her: an access door to the stairs that descended into subterranean corridors. Though reserved for custodians and faculty, students often used them during the winter. The doors were usually left unlocked. Therese refused to think *this* one might be locked. It would open. It *had* to.

Her fingers closed on the handle and she jerked it open. Hope soared at the sight of the door below. If she could reach it, get through and jam it shut somehow ...

Her right foot hit the first step ... and slipped. The world tilted as she pitched downward. The thing's rumble filled the stairwell, and even as she spun away into darkness, she recognized the bubbling sound for what it was.

Laughter.

Chapter Twenty-One

As he charged, Hiram calculated quickly. Fortune smiled upon him. The aisle offered limited room. As the first two beasts slammed tables aside, the third Tanara'ri brought up the rear.

Perfect.

Tentacles snapped as he bent backward and slid feet first on the floor between them and past their fleshy whips. Once clear, he slammed his heels down, sat up and jammed both flares backward. Necrotic flesh burned and glistening fluids spurted.

The monsters screamed and their tentacles beat the air. He scrambled to his feet, reached into his satchel and drew another flare. He snapped it alight and with a roar plunged it deep into the oncoming Tanara'ri's belly. Driving hard with his shoulder, he twisted the flare as they slammed to the floor. The Tanara'ri bucked until something exploded wetly inside, spraying Hiram with black guts. He slid off the still-spasming beast while the others shrieked. One must have ripped the flare out and was now rushing at him. The ground shook with each step.

Hiram rolled until he touched the Franchi's case. He unlatched it, stood and brought the shotgun with him. The Tanara'ri kept coming. For this, he was happy.

He pulled the trigger.

Bluish-orange flame punched the custom-made slug into the closest leathery gut. It exploded into wet chunks. For good measure, he blasted the dying Tanara'ri next to him, also.

A shrill scream. Hiram spun and swore.

Stemmins. He'd forgotten all about the man. What he saw made his blood freeze. The remaining Tanara'ri had retreated, snagging the forgotten vice-provost along the way. Stemmins flailed. As he watched, a thick tentacle reared back and punched downward, tearing into Stemmins' guts. The man bucked and vomited blood. The tentacle pulsed and pumped something into him.

The Hive buzzed in Hiram's mind. They were coming.

"*Dammit!*" He'd no choice. The man was—had been—an asshole, but what was happening to him now, Hiram wished on no one. Still ... there was nothing he could do. Rage burning, Hiram strained against the Hive's pressure and backed out the door. Leveling the Franchi, he pulled the trigger ... and saw the glimmering thanks in Stemmins' eyes as their light faded.

The shotgun bucked against his shoulder as he fired again. The Dragon's Breath flame threw everything into sharp relief.

Hiram turned away as the last Tanara'ri exploded. He didn't need to see anymore.

Stopping for only a quick breath, he dug into his pocket for the EM scanner, pulled it out and re-calibrated it campus-wide. Satisfaction bloomed when the indicator blipped a pale yellow, revealing another source of confluent energy nearby.

"Fantastic." He pocketed the device. "That's got to be it—unless someone *else* on this blasted campus has been summoning sex demons." He sighed. "One disaster at a time, old boy. One disaster at a time."

A woman screamed and a cry of rage bounced off the walls.

Turning, Hiram raised his weapon and braced himself for whatever hurtled around the corner.

Chapter Twenty-Two

Therese landed hard, an aching jumble of arms and legs. Her backpack had twisted around in her fall, got jammed into her face. She desperately shrugged it off.

The Tanara'ri jigged after her. Deafening screeches echoed in the stairwell. Somehow, she gathered her wits, flipped onto her back and reached inside herself, seeking that strange white river. She found it; brimming, surging … waiting. With a scream, Therese lashed out and caught the monster midair with waves of power.

The beast shrieked and thrashed against invisible bonds, but she didn't yield. As its rage grew, a strange calm filled her. She'd never felt anything like it before. Her mind split. There was old Therese: quiet and withdrawn, but there was a *new* Therese—one that felt cold, merciless. Both new and old Therese regarded this thing and realized with fierce pleasure that *It* could be caught, burned … and *destroyed*.

"You *killed* Reggie." Her voice thundered in the stairwell. Barely restrained rage throbbed in her head. Power crackled at her fingertips. "*You killed Reggie!*"

The leathery thing fought and glared. She clenched her fingers, wrapped glittering bands of energy around *It*, and squeezed. "*WHY?*"

It roared and pushed back at Therese with a churning wave of darkness. Her skin crawled, but she held on, though her grip loosened. A slow, rumbling buzz filled her mind. *WE WERE SUMMONED. BOUND TO SIX. WE FED.*

"Why me? I didn't do anything!"

IT MATTERS NOT. WE WERE SUMMONED, BOUND. NOW WE FEED.

Disgust filled her. "So you're like dogs, then. Dogs that chase cars and don't even know why."

WE BELONG. YOU DO NOT. YOU ARE AN ABOMINATION.

"Bullshit!" She tensed her fingers. Power coursed through them. *Its* skin quivered.

NO. YOU ARE A CONSTRUCT. A FABRICATION. NOT REAL.

Her control slipped. Her lower back protesting, Therese slid to her knees and stood, hand still outstretched. She wobbled on unsteady legs but fought to keep her hold. "I don't believe you!"

IT MATTERS NOT.

A chill ran up her spine. Something large rushed towards them. A buzzing rose and fell in her mind. She'd been played a fool, held here in a stalemate until more could arrive. She looked at the creature, her worst fears confirmed. The thing seemed larger. Tentacles snapped and curled with renewed vigor. Her power, however, flickered. She felt the white river ebb, the wall inside rebuilding.

She shuddered. Her hold slipped more. Sweat coated her face. Her head pounded with the strain, legs weak. Anger melted into fear, leaving her powerless.

"You *knew*. You were just waiting."

It blinked and rolled its eyes. *BALANCE MUST BE KEPT. WE MUST FEED. YOU DO NOT BELONG.*

She bumped into the door behind her. She grasped her wrist and braced herself, as if that would help. It didn't. "How? How is that possible?"

WE HAVE PURPOSE. YOU DO NOT.

"*No!*"

Invisible hands clawed at her mind. She looked upward and saw several dark, hulking forms clambering down the stairs. Dead human faces leered.

The final brick fit into place. The wall inside her rose and the power faded once more.

Therese spun, yanked the door open, flung herself through, and ran for all her worth. A dull *boom* echoed as the door slammed open. Shrieks reverberated behind her. Therese's fear spiked, but she didn't look back. She ran, her existence narrowed to surging adrenaline, pounding heart, breathless fear. She braced herself on the wall as she scrambled around the corner, pursued by screams and slapping tentacles.

She heard something, like a shotgun pumping; then *he* rose: the man from *Jimmy's*, pointing a gun at her: Her dreams made real.

"Get down!"

Without hesitation, Therese dove.

# Chapter Twenty-Three

Hiram didn't look as Therese flew by, trusting she'd land safely. Instead, he aimed at the adult Tanara'ri leading the way.

It was massive and quick. Patches of its hide looked scorched. Without a human husk, it moved quicker than its hybrid-brethren, though they, too, lurched with frightening speed. Hiram waited for the right moment, aiming for the apex of its next bounce … and pulled the trigger. Thick tentacles lashed out and pushed off the wall, launching it clear from his shot, which blew a smoking hole in concrete.

Panning across the hall, he fired twice; gutting the hosts lumbering towards them. Flaming chunks of necrotic tissue flew as he spun and tracked the adult Tanara'ri. Quicker than he could follow, it bounced off wall and floor, then slammed into him. Both fell, the Abyssal-spawn on top, Hiram on bottom, the Franchi jammed deep into its gut. The Tanara'ri squealed and tried to wriggle off. Its many eyes widened.

"Sorry. All out of helpless today. Try again tomorrow, perhaps?" The beast keened. Hiram grinned and pulled the trigger.

The empty *clack* thundered. Both man and monster froze, considering the implications.

"Oh, *bollocks*."

The Tanara'ri blinked and rumpled with deep, wet laughter.

"Indeed? See how funny *this* is, you soggy …"

Light filled the hallway and a great wind blew over them. Deathly peace claimed Hiram as he stared, eyes wide, jaw slack in amazement.

The monster screeched as Therese yanked it off him and held it high. Energy swirled and crackled upon her skin. Her face and cobalt blue eyes looked cold, empty. The Tanara'ri struggled in her grip, but it seemed smaller, its essence drained. Through her aura, Hiram heard the creature's thoughts.

NO! ABOMINATION!

She shook the Tanara'ri. "No. *You* are an abomination. *You. Are. Impure.*"

IT IS THE WAY!

A disgusted smiled cracked Therese's mask. "Not anymore."

Hiram eased away, crouched against the wall, and fumbled in his satchel.

CANNOT UPSET BALANCE!

Something terrible glimmered in her smile. "*I* am balance now."

Transfixed by her cold beauty, Hiram dug another magazine from the bag and reloaded the Franchi. Therese's voice intoned, emotionless, "I can burn it down. Make things pure. I'll start … with you."

He pulled the Webley from its holster, flipped the cartridge chamber open, ejecting the standard rounds. Moving slowly, eyes never leaving Therese's transformed face, he reached into the satchel and withdrew a speed-loader, filled with the special iron slugs Bothwell had supplied. As he loaded the Webley, he wondered what the hell he was going to do next.

Chapter Twenty-Four

Darkness. She hated it. It lurked everywhere, and its hunger never faded. All it did was consume and destroy. As Therese's heart throbbed with the white river, she pushed out waves of light against the darkness around them. She would destroy it. She would cleanse the world, make it pure and empty.

She squeezed the Thing in her hand. "Die," she whispered, pouring the white river into it. Cracks glowed in its hideous flesh. She filled it with pure white fire. It shuddered once, then burnt through and exploded. Pieces of blazing tissue flew outward, then faded into the ether.

The darkness was gone. She'd made it pure. Peace settled over her, a sense of justice that she'd never known. Still—the thing's brethren remained. Many surged towards them now.

Therese smiled. She'd destroy them, too. Then, the world would be next. The darkness must be purged, no matter where it hid. *All* must be purged, until everything was empty and pure.

Something *clicked* in her mind. She turned and gazed at the man she now knew to be called Hiram. She could see so much now. In him, too, lurked darkness, along with self-loathing. Despair. Hatred. And something else, oily life, growing in his belly. She reached out, the white river curling at her fingertips. "Hiram …"

Grimacing, he pointed his gun at her. "I'm sorry, love. Please— *don't* move. Not another step."

She frowned as the river surged within.

Hiram aimed the Webley at a spot between Therese's eyes, finger tensed on the trigger, Franchi in his other hand. A buzzing alarm sounded in his head. More Tanara'ri were coming. They didn't have much time.

Which was fabulous, really, because he had no idea what to do.

Therese broke the impasse. "You feel so much pain." Her voice resonated with power. "So much darkness. I can take that away; give you peace." In spite of the Webley, she took another step closer. "With your help, I can make it all go away. No more darkness. No more Abyss."

Hiram tightened his grip on the Webley. His stomach twisted. *Think of it. Lives spared. No more hunting. Destroy evil, rid the world of darkness.*

Bring back Sadie and Mother.

He felt so damn tired. He spent his days drenched in monsters' guts. A dreadful existence, really. The problem? Not all monsters were made of necrotic tissue, conjured by dark magic. Destroying the Abyss wouldn't make monsters disappear.

Hiram shook his head. "You *can't* do that, Therese."

She leaned forward. Her smile shivered, cold and threatening. "Why not?"

Hiram retreated a step. "The Abyss exists for a reason, to maintain balance. That's what *I* do: fight for balance, hold the darkness at bay... not eradicate it. That's not my province. Besides, you can't *have* light without darkness, not in this world." He shook his head. "I don't know how it works, but it does. It's just not for us to decide."

Cobalt blue eyes glowed. "But it could be."

Another shriek, closer this time. The distant pressure of the Hive throbbed against his mind. "We're out of time. If you're in there, Therese, back off. We'll finish this and talk to Mab. Maybe she can help, but right now, switch off the juice or I'll ..."

"Kill me?" She raised frosty-white eyebrows. "Do you really think you can?"

Hiram steadied his hand and thumbed back the hammer. Its echo clanged against his ears. "We'll see, won't we?"

Therese leaned in, arched her eyebrows and whispered, "No, I don't think so. If you could kill me ... you'd have done it already."

The Hive thundered in his head. Sweat poured down his face. The Tanara'ri screamed in his mind, so much closer, and the halls echoed with shrieks and slithering, just around the corner.

Damn you, Mab. He began to squeeze the trigger ...

Therese's aura faded. "What? W-what's happening?"

The light waned and Therese crumpled forward. Hiram spun, caught her in the crook of his arm, raised the Franchi in his other hand, and filled the hallway with fire.

PART 4

Chapter Twenty-Five

Outside

They'd driven in a holding pattern around University Quarter in South Belfast for two hours when a slight tremor shook the streets and buildings. All traffic grounded to a halt. Pedestrians shouted and ran. Distant sirens trilled. Mrs. Bothwell flipped opened her cell phone and hit a number on speed dial.

"*Constable Billings.*"

"Billings, this is Bothwell. How goes the good fight?"

"*A bit hectic. Got a situation at University Quarter. Sounds like a low-grade explosion. Place is in a bloody panic.*"

"Yes, that's why I'm calling."

"*That so? What am I dealin' with?*"

"At the moment, you're not quite sure. It's all speculation, of course. I imagine your best hypothesis would be the Real IRA, though no cell has claimed responsibility yet."

"*That all?*"

"Of course, you're not ruling out an international terrorist attack."

"*Right.*" A pause. Pencil scratched paper. "*Anything else?*"

"It could be something different entirely, like Columbine or Virginia Tech, though you desperately hope not."

"*Sincerely. Now—what do you need?*"

Bothwell smiled at Billings' quick compliance. "Get your most circumspect men and evacuate the campus ASAP. When I'm apprised of the situation, I'll call so your men can stay out of the way."

"*Right. How bad is this?*"

"Hard to tell. There's a contagion threat."

"*Oh, hell. I hate those.*"

"As do I. In any case, I'll contact you when I know more. Good luck, Constable."

"*Aye.*"

The line clicked dead, and Bothwell shut her phone. "He's a good man, Billings." She regarded milling pedestrians and halted cars. "Easy to work with. Not like most."

"Yes, quite." Alphonse Kline III paused. "Are you worried?"

Bothwell shrugged, but didn't return Kline's gaze in the rearview. "I'd guess Hiram's in the thick, as usual." She offered her driver a thin smile. "Of course I'm worried. It's what I do. Besides, this is Hiram we're talking about. If I wasn't worried about him … well now, *that* would be cause for *real* worry, wouldn't it?"

Kline remained silent. To herself, Bothwell whispered, "So what have you gotten yourself into *this* time, Hiram?"

Chapter Twenty-Six

"Therese ... move!"

Hiram yanked a dazed Therese behind him as the last adult Tanara'ri jigged down the hall. She stumbled and fell, but he couldn't do anything about it as he took aim. One Tanara'ri, one shell left. He'd have no chance to reload.

He targeted its next bounce. At the last moment, a tentacle uncoiled and flicked down to the floor. He held the trigger a heartbeat longer. The creature pushed off and bounced towards the ceiling. Hiram smoothly tracked it. As soon as the Tanara'ri entered his line of sight the Franchi thundered and the Tanara'ri exploded, taking a whole bank of fluorescent lights with it, filling the air with iridescent fireworks. Ceiling tile and glass rained down.

Silence, punctuated only by Therese's gasps. She lay on the floor, curled in the fetal position. Hiram knelt next to her, grasped her shoulder. "Therese? Are you hurt?"

She crawled upright and hugged herself. "I-I don't ... no, no, but I'm cold. Freezing." Her teeth chattered, but from chill or shock he couldn't tell. "Wh-what's ... what's happening?" She looked around, not really seeing. "These ... *things* ... they want to kill me. Why? W-what are they?"

Hiram didn't answer. He quickly checked the scanner. The indicator bar reached across the screen, shading from yellow to vibrant orange. "We're close." He looked up and saw stairs about twenty feet away, at the end of a long phalanx with no doors or corners. An idea sparked. If he could close off this intersection, he could buy some time. First things first, though. He unslung his satchel to reload his weapons. First the Webley, then the Franchi.

"Hiram ..."

He stopped. "Yes?"

"What's happening to me?"

"How much do you remember?"

She shook her head. "Everything, but it's like I watched it through a fog." She paused, rested her chin on her knees. "I remember power. I destroyed them all, except one."

"That explosion ... you?"

"Yes." She frowned and looked away. "At the campus bus terminal. A flash, and it was over. It happened again after I fell down the stairs. I was able to *catch* one of those things. But when you ran out of bullets ... I wanted to burn everything down. Destroy the world." She gazed at him. "*What* is happening to me?"

Hiram set the shotgun down. "Power strips away all sense of right and wrong. All that remains are basic desires." He sighed as he reached into the satchel. "Deep inside, you want justice, a world rid of darkness. Nothing wrong with that. Problem is, the only way to completely destroy darkness—in this world, at least—is to destroy everything."

"You didn't answer me. What's happening to me? What am I becoming?"

His fingers closed around several bricks of C-4. "I can't say for sure. It's not my thing, metaphysics." He pulled the explosives out, set them aside, and rummaged some more.

"And *this* is?"

He shrugged. "Yes. There are nasty things in our world—monsters, if you will—that come from a horrible place: the Abyss, the Black, Kadath, Gehenna, Sheol, Hell ... there are hundreds of names. It's my job to kill them. Send them back. Along the way, I try to protect as many innocents as I can." He paused as dark emotions clogged his throat. "Too often, I fail."

"Sadie. When the power took me, I sensed your thoughts ... your pain." She swallowed. "I'm sorry. It was wrong to look into your head like that."

He sucked in a deep breath as he pulled out a handful of the infrared receivers and emitters for the C-4. "Not your fault."

She nodded, then added, "She was important to you. Almost more important than anyone else … since your mother."

He grinned weakly. "You're going to give my boss a run for her money as an armchair psychologist."

She stared at him. "I offered to cleanse your pain. You refused me." He frowned, not liking her tone, but he let her finish. "Why keep pain like that, if you could be rid of it?"

He sat back on his heels. Why indeed?

He looked at her. "Because it makes me who I am. It makes humans who *we* are. Without pain, all the other feelings we cherish would die. It's all one package, see? Can't be separated. I don't like it. Honestly, I hate it, but here on this plane of existence, eliminating pain would destroy the whole balance of things. Understand?"

She shrugged. "Not at all." He resettled about his work, until she asked, "So, does it always go this badly?"

He grunted. "Not *always*." He paused and frowned, reconsidering. "Though frighteningly often, it does."

She snorted at this, then fell silent for several seconds. Finally, she said, "Hiram, I have to ask you something, and I need the truth." Her irises flashed an icy, cobalt blue. "These monsters you hunt. Am I …"

Hiram's lips tightened as he molded another mound of the plastic explosive. "No. You're not a monster, Therese. You are—or were—a scion of Faerie Kind, chosen to be a Faerie Queen. There were five others chosen also. They're dead. You're next to die, or at least … that's what someone wants."

Therese's eyes clouded over. "When the power took me, it told me about the Faerie and the scions. I thought I was hallucinating."

"No. The Faerie are a pain in the ass, but they're real." He paused.

"Therese, do you have a … keepsake, of sorts? Something left to you by your real parents, a necklace with a charm or something?"

Therese nodded, held out her right hand. A bracelet with its charm slid down her wrist. A quick glance confirmed what he thought: the charm looked exactly like Mab's. "Yes. That's the sigil of Queen Mab. It's also supposed to cloak the Veil within you, but now that you have so much, it's not working."

Therese sat, fingered the charm, staring at it. "I always believed that even though my parents had given me up, one of them cared enough to leave something of themselves with me in this charm. Now, I suppose it's more like a fence to guard a possession, rather than a token of love."

Hiram didn't quite know how to respond, so he chose to avoid it directly. "In any case, it was left by your mother … Queen Mab of Faerie. It's your heritage, I suppose. I imagine you're an artist of sorts?"

"Painter." Therese blinked, as if surprised to be asked something so mundane. "I'm a third-year Art student. Sold a few paintings, here and there. Why do you ask?"

"Apparently, all scions dabble in the arts. It's a reflection of the Veil's beauty inside them. Just satisfying idle curiosity, I suppose."

A moment of silence, until, "Hiram … *will* you have to kill me?"

"No." *Liar.*

"How will you stop these … *things*? Are there people you can call for, like … backup, or something?"

"No, there's just me."

"So how will you …"

"Someone summoned these things, either with a talisman—something used to focus dark magic—or through themselves, which we call a conduit. Either way, summoned entities are bound to them. Destroy the object or eliminate the conduit, break the binding … *poof* … back they go."

"Wait. Eliminate the conduit? But if the conduit's a person, that means you'd have to …"

He nodded but didn't look at her. "Yes."

"Oh." A thoughtful, heavy pause. "And you're tracking them?"

"The little rectangular bit you've seen me carrying, the scanner? That's doing the tracking."

"How?"

Hiram cringed. This part he loathed. "Well, to be honest, some of it … hell, *most* of it … is over my head. I don't like technology. Even these twenty-year-old infrared emitters give me twitches." He shook his head. "Anyway, Bothwell—she's my boss—knows all the particulars. I do the hunting. When these things cross over, it's called a confluence. It generates a lot of power. Not only can we detect that energy and locate a confluence, we can find the talisman or the conduit."

"Because of the energy attached to either."

"Very good. Of course, who would've guessed that on the same campus where Sumerian demons were loping about, a vice-provost would also be summoning succubae for his own perverted distractions?"

"What are *they*?"

"Sex demons. Whores from hell."

Therese raised her eyebrows. "*Oh.* So that's what my roommate was, freshman year. Good to know."

"Quite. That's why I was in the artifacts room. Followed a wrong signal there."

"And what you're tracking now is the right one?"

"Should be, yes. The readings indicate *immense* concentrations of confluential energies."

They fell into a companionable silence as Hiram worked. When he was finished, he planned to detonate the C-4 and block the intersection with rubble. Hopefully, he'd made the right calculations, Bothwell's jests regardless.

"Hiram, I have one more question, then I promise to shut up."

He chuckled. "It's all right, really. It's been a while since ...," something stuck in his throat and hurt. "Well, it's been a while."

A pause, then, "Hiram ... can I trust you?"

He looked up, understanding but reluctant to voice it. "How do you mean?"

"When the time comes, will you do whatever it takes to ... stop me? So I won't *become* a monster?"

His jaw clenched. He'd no real assurances to give, but what could he say? "Promise."

He resumed his work and Therese lapsed into silence. They didn't speak for some time.

Chapter Twenty-Seven

"It's quiet."

Hiram peered down the dimly lit halls. It *was* quiet ... but something didn't feel right. "Yes. Fortuitous, but damned odd."

Still sitting with her knees drawn to her chest, Therese frowned. "Why?"

Hiram prepared another clump of C-4. "According to what I know about these creatures—which isn't much—they're like rats. They replicate, consume: that's what they do. They aren't coming at us as hard as I'd expect."

"This isn't hard?"

"This *has* been horrible, to be sure, but not consistent with their behavior as I understand it. They're supposed to consume everything in their path, stop for nothing. They haven't done that."

"And this *worries* you?"

"Strangely enough, yes. They're attacking us in packs, strategically. They're supposed to overrun. It's too calculating. Methodical. On one hand, it means fewer casualties. I'm all for that."

"But?"

"It means whoever summoned these things has great willpower. I'm not sure which I'm more frightened of: the monsters or their summoner."

"Hmmm. I'm gonna go with monsters."

"For now, I'm inclined to agree. Afterwards ... we'll see."

"If there is an afterwards."

"There will be. One way or another, there will ... wait." Something brushed his mind. The lights flickered, plunging them into darkness, then snapping back again. "What the *hell?*"

Therese went rigid. "My God. What time is it?"

"I've no idea, maybe early evening, by now." The lights faded and rose again. Hiram's head buzzed louder with the voices of the Hive.

Therese staggered upright. "I can't believe I forgot about this …"

He forced his annoyance down. "*Now* would be a good time to educate me!"

Lights off, then on. The Hive buzzed closer.

"The tunnels are on a timer. Lights shut off at five o'clock. There's a flicker delay, so stragglers can get to an exit."

"How long?" The corridor dimmed, lit again.

"Cassie and I got caught down here last year. One more."

"Damn!" He didn't have time. He stuffed the remote detonator in his pocket; the remaining C-4 into the satchel. He grabbed two magnesium flares, gave one to Therese. After a moment's hesitation, he pulled the Webley from its holster and handed it to her.

Therese's face blanched. "Hiram, I can't. I'll never …"

"Take it. No arguments."

She relented. The gun looked ridiculously large in her hands but oddly *right*, somehow. He tried very hard not to paste his mother's face over Therese's.

He dug into the satchel once more. The light flickered on and off. Pulling out utility tape, he lashed the flare alongside the Franchi's barrel. "Pop your flare, before …"

The hall plunged into a swimming, unrelenting darkness. Two sparkling suns erupted, threw strange lights on the walls. The flares hissed and popped. "Back up. This is risky, but I'm blowing the C-4. The sooner I close this hall off, the better."

He glanced at Therese. For a moment, he couldn't help staring. She stood limply, suffused with a soft, effervescent glow. "Therese?"

She looked at him, face slack. Hiram was struck again by how much her eyes looked like Mab's. "Yes. I'm still here."

He licked dry, parched lips, wishing Bothwell had been kind enough to add a flask of whiskey to the supplies she'd brought him. His knees trembled. During their brief respite, the things inside him had fallen still. Now, the Hive swelled all around, and they twitched in response.

Go ahead, say it. Don't mince words now. They might be your last.

"Therese, you asked me to do the right thing." She nodded vacantly. "Well, I'm going to ask you something also. If things go bad in here, if you have to let it out ... do it. Burn us all."

She nodded and closed her eyes. When she opened them, a slight chill ran through him. They glowed cobalt blue. "Indeed." The voice didn't belong to Therese Fitzgerald.

"Right. Shall we?"

Hiram held the Franchi in one hand, dug the remote from his pocket with the other. He stumbled backwards. He wasn't sure how much further he needed to go, at least a few feet ...

Shrieks filled the hall. Hiram spun, thumb on the detonator's switch ...

Therese shouted. A rubbery mass slammed him to the floor. His head struck concrete, filling it with pain and pressure. A tentacle knocked the detonator from his hand. Another wrapped around his neck and squeezed. More shrieks echoed down the hall, and the Hive pounded in his mind: *EAT YOU! EAT YOU!*

Therese screamed and the Webley hammered—once, twice, and then again. Hiram took fierce pleasure in the sound, futile as it was. The Tanara'ri yanked his neck harder and glared at him with impossible, alien eyes. *Eat you slowlyyyyy ...*

Useless rage consumed him. He kicked, felt maggots burning his exposed skin, and fired wildly. He missed, but the Dragon's Breath flame licked the hide of the beast attacking him. It screamed and loosened its hold on his neck. He managed to shift the barrel of the gun and jam it deep into the thing's belly. Roaring, he pulled the trigger, and the Tanara'ri exploded. He rolled away, covered his face, but the flames still tasted his clothes and burnt his skin.

The Webley roared, twice more, then clicked empty on its sixth shot—the phantom suicide shell.

A shriek. Hiram rolled over and fired at a flicker of eyeshine, and another Tanara'ri exploded. Two more filled its place. Hiram fired twice more. They exploded into flaming pieces that scattered light throughout the darkness.

He had only one shot left. He couldn't reach his bag to reload. Shrieks and shuffles and scrambling tentacles surrounded them.

A Tanara'ri lunged at Therese, the gestating host in its belly whipping smaller but still deadly tentacles. Hiram blew it in two. Shotgun now empty, he drew his Pritchard and scrambled to his feet. "Therese! Behind me …!"

A shuddering impact tossed him past her, into the opposite wall. He struck face-first. The world spun as blood poured down his face. The thing on his back screamed—and suddenly vanished. Light exploded all around. Hiram gasped, rolled over and stared.

Therese shimmered as she held the monster above her. Waves of power flowed from her and lit up the halls. Tanara'ri filled the corridor. Full grown adults, gestating young embedded in human husks. They froze at the sight of Therese, transfixed by the light pouring from her as she snarled and twisted her hands deeper into necrotic tissue. As one, they scuttled back into the C-4's blasting path.

"Therese! The C-4! They're under the C-4!"

She shook the beast once as white fire pulsed through it. "Yes!" She wound up and threw the glowing creature at the ceiling.

The world throbbed with fire, light and thunder. A long psychic wail slammed Hiram into oblivion.

Chapter Twenty-Eight

Therese faced her nightmare door. Something felt different. Nothing pursued her. She stood alone. Biting her lip, she grasped the knob. A hollow voice from over her shoulder said, "You can't do this alone."

She turned, and faced herself. The Chosen One's eyes glowed a deep blue. Her smile cut, harsh and cruel. "I'm not waiting forever. Eventually, we're going to have this out."

Therese shook her head. "You don't control me."

"But you can't *control me. You're too weak. Too human."*

Therese turned away. The Chosen One was lying. Therese could control her. She just had to learn how.

"Good luck, sweetie." Heels clicked away in the silent hall. "Call me when you change your mind."

Therese blinked and woke amidst smoking debris.

Sunday Morning

As soon as the automatic lights—those still working—switched on, Hiram woke to a medley of pains. He blinked, but that only brought a fresh wave of agony.

The last time he hurt this badly, he'd consumed liters of absinthe and enjoyed the company of many girls. Dressed as police. With batons. He'd an awful premonition that when he opened his eyes this time, he wasn't going to see any scantily-clad policewomen.

"Oh, hell." Hiram pushed himself up. Vertigo swelled and his stomach churned. He winced and grabbed his head. Closing his eyes, he breathed deeply and the nausea passed, but a twitch—the things inside him—still remained.

Gradually, his headache receded to a dull throbbing. He opened his eyes and took stock of the destruction. The C-4 had done its job well. Rubble blocked off the corridor. Nothing would come through that mess any time soon.

"You're awake."

Hiram glanced over his shoulder; saw Therese standing away from him, holding the scanner. He ran a hand through his hair and winced as he found several bumps and small cuts.

"What do we do now?"

Hiram sighed and rose. "What I do best, love. Figure it out along the way."

The door to the surface loomed before them. Weapons reloaded and ready for whatever lay ahead, Hiram now sagged against the wall. Every few minutes, his lungs rattled with wet coughs. His calves burned, arms shook, and the Franchi felt leaden in his hands.

He rested his head on cool concrete and glanced at Therese, standing next to him, Webley held to her side. Her hair was tangled, clothes soiled. He imagined he looked far worse.

His chest twisted and he doubled over in a hacking fit. Slowly, it passed. He wiped a blood-clotted hand on his trousers and straightened.

"It's getting worse, isn't it?"

He began to object, but when he found Therese's gaze, he stopped. He couldn't lie. "Yes. It is."

"How long?"

"Hard to tell. An hour. Maybe more. Maybe less." He cleared his throat and changed the subject. "So, you've no idea what part of campus this'll bring us to?"

"No clue. The intersections all have arrow systems painted on them," she jerked a thumb over her shoulder, "but … uhm … I think I wrecked that one." A pause. "So, the talisman is past this door?"

He checked the scanner. "Should be. Something nearby is creating *waves* of confluential energy."

"What do you think has happened up there?"

"Hopefully Bothwell achieved containment. I'm sure she came up with something. She cleans up all my messes." He frowned. "Well, most of them."

"Hiram?"

"Yes?"

"Thank you. For everything. I don't know what I'm trying to say, really, except …"

He nodded. Sucked in a deep, steadying breath. "Likewise." More silence, something almost like peace, until Hiram waved a hand at the door. "It's all yours, love. Be my guest."

Therese nodded, raised the Webley, and pulled the trigger. It roared in the confines of the tunnel as she blew away the door's lock. He led the way and she followed into the shadows beyond.

Chapter Twenty-Nine

Hiram quickly lit the new flare affixed to the Franchi and led Therese into a cramped custodian's office. A single light bulb hung from the ceiling. He pulled its cord, and the room sprang into sickly, orange gloom. They crept forward. Hiram noted shelves packed with spare parts, a pegboard off which a variety of pedestrian tools hung, and an oil-spotted, grungy metal desk to their right, pushed against the wall. Paper littered the desk's top, of the usual sorts: 'to do' lists, purchase orders and receipts, memos.

Apparently, this custodian fancied himself a handyman-philosopher. Several books sat on the desk's corner: *Leaves of Grass*, *Walking*, a collection of Rumi's poetry, even Sun-Tzu. Atop the books, of all things, sat an origami bull. His gaze lingered upon it.

"Hiram..."

A slight gust blew the far door ajar. They froze. Nothing moved, there was no sound. After several more seconds, they approached the door. Hiram probed the opening with the Franchi and its sputtering flare. Nothing. He pushed it open. A short stairwell led up. Sunlight crept down from above. Hiram entered the doorway, held out his hand. Soft wind caressed his skin.

"It's so still, like nothing's left alive except ... us."

Hiram tilted his head. "Maybe Bothwell evacuated the place, saved thousands of lives."

"Or maybe there's no one left to save."

Hiram nodded. "There's always that, too."

He leaned out as far as he dared, tried to see the floor above, but save some greenish wallpaper, a ceiling fan and rafters, he saw nothing except a brown, leathery object at the top of the stairs.

He squinted. A shoe. On a foot, twisted at an odd angle.

His chest spasmed. He ducked back into the custodian's office to stifle his cough. For the most part, he was successful, but the pain ... a tightness burned across his chest, like steel bands wound around his heart. The Hive pulsed on the edge of his thoughts. He couldn't tell if it came from nearby, or from the things inside him.

The spasms eased. He sighed, leaned on the door frame, and closed his eyes. Flushed and chilled, he both sweated and shivered at once.

Damn you. Move your ass up those stairs ... now.

He swallowed. Licked his lips. Opened his eyes and assessed the stairwell. He didn't like it. Too narrow. If they were attacked while climbing, they'd have little room to move. There was no other way, however.

He checked the scanner. The indicator light burned deep orange, almost red. The summoning talisman had to be above. He stepped back into the doorway, pocketed the scanner, ripped the flare off the Franchi, and tossed it into the stairwell. Reaching into his satchel, he gathered the remainder of his supplies—a magazine, a speed-loader, and the last brick of C-4—and pocketed them. He withdrew the last four flares, tossing the now empty bag aside, and lit them all in turn. With an underhanded lob, he pitched them onto the upper landing. They spun—spitting, hissing, bright little suns—up and over the railing, each landing with a light clatter. They rolled and came to sputtering rests.

Nothing. No hisses, no slithering. Silence loomed, save the crackling of the flares. He nodded to Therese, and they ascended. Each step took momentous will. His calves cramped, his temples ached.

The smell hit near the top. Behind him, Therese gasped. A rank miasma of decay bloomed as they stepped onto the first floor. The object at the top of the stairs was indeed a shoe, the foot inside, however, only extended to a ragged mess about mid-ankle. Flies and ants crawled everywhere.

"Sweet mother …" He heard Therese gag and vomit, presumably back down the stairs.

Dismembered bodies littered the floor. Gnawed limbs strewn about. Maybe ten corpses; maybe fifteen or twenty. He couldn't be sure, not with such a jumble of discarded body parts and glistening wet meat.

The stink of spoiled blood and greasy bodily gases saturated the air. Therese staggered back to his side. For a brief moment, she looked ready to vomit again. "My God. It's so *horrible*."

Hiram stepped over the severed foot and picked his way through spilled innards and pooling juices. He stepped on something rubbery. He gazed down, and even *his* stomach swirled as intestines squelched under his shoe.

"Those things inside you … will they become…?"

Hiram shook his head, kept the Franchi up as he stepped past what was either a shredded young girl or two girls sludged together. "No. Not enough in me, I don't think. They're doing considerable damage, though."

He consulted the scanner, looked down the hall to his left. "Not this way." He turned the opposite direction. The indicator bar turned red. "Down this hall, on the right."

They turned. He immediately regretted it. The body count loomed higher this way, with piles of intact, bloated corpses. Horrible, death-frozen screams contorted the faces.

Therese inhaled sharply. "Yes," he murmured. "Horrible, isn't it?"

Therese grabbed his arm. "That's not it. Hiram, are you sure that thing is reading right?"

Hiram frowned. "Yes. It should be down that hall, through the doorway at the end, I think."

"Hiram, the wall. Over the community bulletin board, near those chairs and plants. It says …"

" … Whitaker Hall, I see that. I'm not sure I …"

"Whitaker Hall." She looked at Hiram, her lips shivering. "These are the upperclassmen rooms, next to the nature preserve. My *home*."

Her eyes widened, glinting a faint cobalt blue. "My home, Hiram. Why are we in my home?"

Chapter Thirty

"Hiram," Therese persisted, "why are we here? How can that thing ... the talisman ... be in my home?"

"I don't know. Let me think ... wait." He examined the corpses, every detail. "Therese, if you live here ... don't you know these people?"

"I ... no. No, I don't. Some of them are so ... gone ... it's hard to tell, but the others," she waved at the piles of bloated corpses, "they don't live here."

"They were brought here, then, because ..."

Something splattered amidst the piles of intact bodies. The dead jiggled. The room's stench worsened as gases trapped in bloated bellies spilled into the air. Therese's eyes widened as bodies quivered and deflated.

"*God.* That's horrible. Do corpses always do that?"

Hiram frowned. He gripped the Franchi tighter. "Occasionally, but something's not cricket ..." Wet sounds ripped along the bodies in rapid succession.

"Hiram, *what's happening?*"

He pieced it together. On one side, mangled piles of melted flesh; on the other, preserved, bloated corpses, waiting for ...

A memory surfaced, of a tentacle punching into Vice-provost Stemmins' gut, pumping and pulsing ... something *into him* ...

"Oh, *hell.* We're in a lot of trouble." One side was a desecrated trough—a feeding ground. The other side, however, bodies preserved and whole ...

"What is it?"

He aimed at the corpses, but he'd no idea where to fire first. "It's a nest, Therese. A damned nest."

A thin tentacle—only the width of an index finger, but repulsive all the same—burst from one of the distended bellies closest to them with a soggy tearing sound. A high-pitched squeal pierced Hiram's head as Tanara'ri younglings screamed in newborn hunger.

Chapter Thirty-One

Thin tentacles punched through rotten flesh. Younglings squealed. Therese pointed the Webley everywhere, arms shaking. "What do we do? Will they …?"

"I wouldn't bet against it." He winced. "I can *hear them* … calling to the things inside me …" Hiram set his teeth as he dug into his pockets. "We have to get through, Therese. Whatever we do, we have to get to that room at the end of the hall."

"That's my room, Hiram! Mine!"

"We'll sort that out when we get there." His fingers closed around his last brick of C-4. "Somehow, you're the center of all this. This whole thing has been about you from the very start."

He pressed the C-4 into a lopsided sphere, watching the field of tentacles struggle amidst melted flesh. His stomach lurched, thinking of snakes writhing and twining around one another.

"Hiram, whatever you're doing, please … there's more of them coming out. *God*, holy *shite* …"

A ripping sound. Something flipped and writhed in viscous fluids. "Hiram … they're getting free! *What* are you doing?"

"Well, I'm either going to blow a path through, or blow us to hell. I've never been that good with C-4."

"*What?*"

He tossed the ball into the air once. "If I don't blow us to hell … run. Don't stop. I'll follow and cover. Just run, hard as you can. I imagine once this starts, it won't be long until Mama and Papa show their ugly heads. They're probably coming already."

Therese nodded once. She held the Webley out to him. "Take it."

Hiram frowned. "Love, you'll be defenseless …"

"I'll be running, not shooting." Something flashed in her eyes. "It'll slow me down."

Hiram saw the icy blue in her eyes and nodded. He palmed the C-4 and hooked the outstretched Webley's trigger guard with a finger. He felt horrible leaving Therese weaponless, but couldn't deny a flush of satisfaction at having his faithful revolver back.

He holstered the Webley. "Now, get ready to …"

An enormous, fleshy belch interrupted him. A chorus of squeals pierced his mind. Tentacles snapped and thudded against dead flesh. A small crater had blown outward from one of the bodies. Dozens—perhaps more—of Tanara'ri younglings surged forth.

"Here it is." He tossed the C-4 underhand. It flew in a shallow arc, then descended. Hiram raised the Franchi and waited. Slowly at first, then with gathering intensity, the air around them rippled. Power flowed off Therese and lapped against him, like soft eddies in a stream.

The explosive landed amongst surging Tanara'ri newborn. "Right then. Tally-fucking-ho."

The fire and shock wave of the Franchi's special round set off the C-4, and the resulting explosion dug a jagged trench through the corpses. Younglings blew to pieces. A unified screech filled the air. Knocked off balance, Therese fell. Hiram went down, as well, sprawling onto crushed bodies. Somehow, he held onto the shotgun. Struggling to his knees, face pinched and flushed, he gestured at the burning trench. "Go!"

Therese slipped in blood as she scrambled upright, ignoring the fleshy clumps sticking to her legs. She tensed to push off when something crashed. Adult Tanara'ri bounded through the front doors.

Gestating hybrids scrambled behind. Hiram shot the first creature, blew it in two. Three more took its place.

A throbbing drone pounded her brain: *FEED, FEED, FEED!*

"Run, dammit! *Run!*" Another Tanara'ri exploded. Another *clack*, another blast. "*RUN!*"

She vaulted over a half-eaten torso and sprinted towards the cleared path. Her legs pumped, feet pounded. Something stirred inside. Fueled by white fire and dark pain, Therese ran, while explosions thundered all around. Fire raged and monsters screamed.

A great picture window to her right shattered into thousands of jagged shards. She ducked as she ran, but glass still sliced her hands and cheeks. A Tanara'ri had burst through the window. Therese ran harder, fueled by panic … but it didn't pursue her. It screeched, tentacles snapping.

There was a rush of air and Hiram sailed high overhead. He smashed into the glass-covered bulletin board and rolled to the floor in a shower of broken shards, still clutching the Franchi. He didn't rise, however. He shuddered on the ground, blood quickly soaking through his jacket at one shoulder.

Therese scrambled over smoking corpses to him. He moaned, his breath shallow, reedy.

"Hiram! Get up! *Please*, get up!" A horrible coldness filled her belly. Where his suit darkened with blood, a jagged piece of glass poked out. Hiram tried to rise, but his arms shivered and he collapsed again.

Therese closed her eyes. She ignored the oncoming beasts and the younglings squirming all around, blocked out their minds, which buzzed against hers. Blindly, she reached down and yanked the shard from Hiram's shoulder.

He screamed, his cries mingling with those of the hungry.

Chapter Thirty-Two

Pain blazed through Hiram's body and mind, muffled the buzz of the Hive. A mixed blessing, because it hurt like hell.

"Hiram, please! We're going to die if you don't move!"

"Right, love. Let's get on that." Breathing deeply, he pushed himself to his knees. He bit his tongue to keep from screaming, and a coppery taste filled his mouth. His head throbbed. A Tanara'ri—a big one—had crashed through a window, caught him by the neck. He'd fired; there'd been a lurch ... then a rush of wind. Impact. Shattering glass, and an explosion of pain in his right shoulder. Then he'd fallen. Now, here he was: on his knees, bleeding all over, wrenched with pain.

"Come on, then. I'm Hiram Grange. This is what I *do*, dammit."

He staggered upright, leaned on Therese for support. They turned and faced the advancing wall of writhing tentacles and blinking eyes. The Hive screamed in his head. Hiram sagged, almost collapsed. Somehow, Therese spun them away, down the hall.

Therese lugged Hiram forward. The calls of the Tanara'ri faded. Nothing existed for her but that *door* at the hallway's end. She'd feared it all her life, but the time had come. She needed to see what lay on the other side. She was no longer afraid.

Hiram slipped off her shoulder and staggered on his own. She sprinted forward, grabbed the knob, twisted, slammed the door with her shoulder ... it was *locked*. She always locked it, of course, and her keys ...

... were gone. She'd jammed them into the Reggie-thing's eye. They'd been destroyed.

Somehow Hiram rallied enough strength to limp along on his own. A psychic pressure pounded him from behind. Ahead, Therese slammed into the door. She jerked the knob, slammed it again.

"It's locked!" She looked at him, face wild. "I lost my keys back at the bus terminal!"

He aimed and pulled the trigger—the Franchi was empty. He grabbed the last magazine from his pocket, slapped it in. A wasted shot, he knew, but without shelter, one more bullet wouldn't matter.

"Move!"

Therese's eyes widened. She jumped clear.

In the close quarters, the shotgun roared. The doorknob blew apart and hot shrapnel bounced off floor, walls and ceiling. Tiny bits burned his cheeks. The Tanara'ri screamed behind them.

Therese leaped to her feet. "How will we close it?"

"Do you have chalk and some salt?"

"What?"

"Do you have them?"

"Yes, but I don't …"

"Get them! NOW!"

She ran into the room. Hiram turned, ignored the burning pain in his shoulder, and took aim. The narrowed hallway had bottlenecked the Tanara'ri, which gave him some time, but not much. He was nearing the end, he knew. Five more shots. Then nothing. It would have to do.

He aimed and fired. The hall filled with heat and greenish flame as a Tanara'ri exploded. Charred remains clogged the hall, forcing the others to slow down. One of the creatures scrambled over its dead fellow, eyes bulging as it screeched. Hiram waited for it to crest the remains. When it did, he fired, adding to the wall of necrotic tissue.

A smaller Tanara'ri bounced off the wall and flew at him, tentacles snapping. Hiram shot and missed, hit the ceiling. Spongy tile blew apart, lights shattered. He fired again, hit the mark. Oily chunks sprayed him.

A heartbeat had passed. Only one shot remained. He fired, and blasted another scampering over the pile. More dead added to the barrier, for whatever it was worth.

He pulled the trigger, just to be certain. It *clacked* empty.

Side-hand, he whipped the Franchi at the closest beast, not bothering to watch it bounce off the leathery hide. He spun into Therese's where she waited, face white, hands shaking. In one hand a jar full of chalk, in the other a bag of cooking salt. He grabbed the salt, spilled half its contents in the door's opening, then swept the jar to the floor, where it shattered. He knelt, snatched a piece of chalk, glanced up as another of the creatures clambered over its dead fellows, and quickly drew an arc between both sides of the door frame, closing a circuit around the spilled salt.

"What are you doing?"

He etched frantic symbols. "Magic! Pisses me off, but I've no other choice!"

"Magic? Why the *hell* didn't you use it before?"

He scribbled a hexagram. "I only know the basics: wards, second sight and such. Plus ... I'm not very good at it!"

"Will it work?"

"Every home has a protective aura. That's why some beings can't come in uninvited. Can't pass through the aura. Wards taps into that aura. This *should* work." He paused, then drew another symbol. "I hope so, anyway."

"You *hope* so?!"

"I'm certain it will. Probably!"

Finished, he sat back and checked his work. It cut things razor close, but if he forgot something, he'd never have another chance. Hexagrams in three cardinal directions: north, south, east. Interspersed between them were two pentagrams. At the north: a hasty caricature of the Tanara'ri. Encompassing everything, a Sumerian Binding Triangle. It was all there. Crude, sloppy, but it'd have to do.

He rose, drew his Pritchard from its sheath, and faced north. As a Tanara'ri lunged, he gripped cold, naked steel. With a jerk, he slashed the tender meat of his palm. It burned, but he used the pain to focus his will. He closed his eyes, breathed ... and time slowed. He blocked out the cries of the surging Hive, focused on Therese, sought the essence imbued in this place she called home.

The monster crossed the threshold. Hiram held his hand over the salt and squeezed blood into the half-circle. "Eteru, nisiqtu, *ENIR!*"

Shafts of white fire flowed around the chalk semi-circle, extended to the ceiling, snaring the Tanara'ri mid-leap. A sour, burnt odor filled the room. The creature writhed and screeched.

Hiram scooped up the bag of salt and faced the glowing barrier. "*Exuro, exussum ... Girru kadingir!*"

He hurled salt at the white fire, which transformed the expanding crystals into waves of silvery-blue flames. The Tanara'ri twitched once and exploded. The white inferno surged down the hall and incinerated everything in its path. Tanara'ri—adult, gestating, young— vaporized. It reached the length of the hall before it stopped. Everything burned, purified by white fire. Hordes of Abyss-spawn screamed beyond the flames.

A magical backlash slammed Hiram in the chest and knocked him to the floor. Breathless, he rose onto his elbows and whistled. "*Kali's tit!* How the hell did I do that?"

Therese looped an arm under his, pulled him to his knees. "I thought you said you weren't any good?"

He shook his head. Weakness assaulted him, and his heart

thudded sluggishly. "I'm ... not. That spell's generic, designed to use any household aura. We owe those flames to you."

She frowned. "What do you mean?"

"Well," he gestured around the room, "I imagine this is where you paint? Where you've been channeling your visions from the Veil?"

A pause, then a reluctant, "Yes."

He nodded. "Makes sense. The Veil abounds here, makes tossing magic around like throwing a match into a gas tank."

"How long do we have?"

He shook his head. "Not long. Even with all that power, the fire is fading." He nodded down the hall. The blue-white flames had weakened. "Before long, they'll crowd and press against the barrier, wear it down. I don't have the strength to keep recasting the spell."

"We need to find that talisman, right?" Therese's head jerked around, eyes searching. "What would it look like?" She moved away from him. "How will we know when ..."

He grabbed her arm, gently but firmly. "Therese ... that's all changed."

She stared at him. "Why?"

He paused, not wanting to voice it, though he knew he had to. "Therese, I don't think any one thing in this room caused the confluence. It was channeled through here, yes ... but not with a talisman."

Therese shook her head. "What? Are you saying these beasts came through here? Through my *home?*"

"Not necessarily. Given the power available here, and someone who knew what they were doing, they could've opened the door here, then ushered them through the Veil anywhere they wanted." He paused. "There were medallions, Therese—sent to each girl as a marker, I believe. Whoever did this most likely directed the confluential energies at the medallions."

"A medallion." A sorrowful expression drained Therese's face. "I got one—horrible thing—in the mail. Reggie thought it was a gift from a secret lover …"

Her eyes widened. "Oh, *God*. The medallion … he kept it, because I wouldn't touch it!"

Pieces fit together at last. "Ah. That explains the day's lag in the Binding."

She covered her face with her hands. "I killed him, then. I killed Reggie."

"*No*, not you, Therese. Someone else did this, broke in here, summoned these things. You couldn't have known. It's not your fault."

"How? How did someone break in here; how did I miss it?"

"Whoever did this knew about the faerie scions, something *no one* knows about. In comparison, breaking in here would've been child's play."

She gasped. "The night of those other deaths … I *wasn't* here! I was at Cassie's house. When I stumbled in last night … wait."

"What is it?"

"On the floor, by the window … that rug." She looked at Hiram. "I rolled it up Thursday morning, wanted to get a frayed corner fixed. I kept tripping on it. Reggie was going to …" She swallowed. "Take it for me. It's unrolled now. Didn't notice the other night, because I collapsed right into bed."

He glanced at the rug, back at her. He limped over to it. Therese followed. For a moment, they just stared. The rug looked worn, innocuous, faded and threadbare. Sure enough, one of its corners frayed upward.

The ward around the door hummed, muffled the Hive's shrieks.

Hiram peered closer. Red streaks peeked out from under the frayed corner. He tapped it with his shoe and nodded at Therese. He knelt and drew back the rug.

Beneath it were three circles, drawn one within the other, large enough for any man to sit cross-legged. Inscribed across them were numerous, complex symbols, far more intricate than the ones Hiram had just drawn. In the very center, painted in some kind of thick, red paste—dried blood—was a horrifyingly familiar symbol.

A circle cut through with a lightning bolt. On one side, a book and quill. On the other, three dots, representing three crystals.

Hiram looked up, felt hollow in his bones. "This … is a problem."

Chapter Thirty-Three

"W-what do you mean?"

Quiet stretched between them. Hiram grappled with an unfamiliar sensation: Helplessness. "Therese ..." he sagged. "There's no summoning talisman to destroy. No goblet or charm or dagger. These things weren't conjured with Dark Magic, they were conjured with the power of the Veil ... with *your power.*" He pointed at the Summoning Circle on the floor. "That's the sigil of Mab, the same as on your charm."

She stared at the Circle. "You mean ..."

He hated himself for even thinking it. "Yes. For all intents and purposes, *you* are the conduit."

She pulled from his grasp and hugged herself, looking at the floor. The protective ward around the door sputtered. Beyond, the shrieks grew louder.

He ran his sliced hand through scraggly hair, unheeding of the bloody streaks left behind. He felt small. "I don't know what to do."

Her eyes blazed as she looked at him. "I do."

His emotions surged, but before he could speak, Therese raised her palm. "Please. There isn't anything more you *can* do. I see that now." Her eyes flashed cobalt blue. Though her voice wavered, it was underscored by an iron regality Hiram found moving and frightening; it reminded him of Mother.

"*You* have to kill me, Hiram. Eliminate the conduit, right?"

"No." His head pounded as the ward weakened more, and the Hive's psychic tendrils leaked through. "There's got to be another way."

"Hiram, what choice do we have? Do *you* have? No offense, but you look awful. You can't do any more." She paused, her voice cooling. "When the power comes again, I won't be able to stop it."

Something tickled in his chest, the things inside him awakening as the Hive's presence in the room grew stronger. He didn't want to admit it, but truth hummed in Therese's words. Still, he shook his head and felt a familiar anger rising inside. "No. You *can't* ask me to do this, dammit." He inspected the Summoning Circle, plying his knowledge for a clue, anything—a catch or loophole. As he scanned symbols he didn't recognize, he protested, "I've never *seen* anything like this before. How can someone be made into a remote conduit? It's preposterous!"

"Hiram, please. Me for them. Sound familiar? Balance."

"NO!" He stalked towards her, jabbing a finger. "No! Don't believe that Faerie balance shit! It's just their way of pretending they know more than us, when they don't know anything!"

He stopped and faced her, nose to nose. "I won't do it. It's contrived nonsense."

Therese didn't blink. "Hiram, it's not nonsense. You know it. That's why you're so angry."

"We'll find another way."

"How?" she gestured at the flickering ward. "In minutes, the spell will fall. They'll kill you, and when that happens, I'll lose control." Her eyes flashed, cold and remote. "I'll become a monster, and you won't be around to stop me."

Pain shot through his temples, but he refused to yield. "No. I can't."

Therese took his face into her hands; they felt burning cold. "Hiram ... I've been dreaming of this my whole life." Her eyes flicked to something over his shoulder. "Of course. Now I see."

He turned, following Therese's gaze. He froze when he saw it, standing in the corner of her living room. Nothing more than an easel, of course—to be expected in an artist's home. It stood there, normal as can be, covered by an old drop cloth. When his eyes fell upon it, however, the whole world went away. There was no more Therese, no more Tanara'ri … no more things burrowing in his chest. There was him, the cloaked easel, and nothing else.

"Go, Hiram. See the truth."

He pulled himself free from Therese's grip and approached the easel. He barely felt himself moving, scarcely felt the rough texture of the cloth as he pulled it away. The screams outside grew louder. He touched the painting, felt the dry brush strokes. As he traced their lines, *understanding* blossomed. He turned and looked at Therese with a heavy heart—her face so unlike his Mother's or Sadie's, but very much the same. Mab had told him, but he hadn't wanted to believe. Now he had no choice.

"I'm so sorry, love."

"Hiram, remember. You *promised*. The right thing, no matter what."

He tipped his head and smiled bitterly. "I know, love. I know." He drew the Webley and fired.

A horrible rose bloomed over her heart. She flew back into the bookshelf, hit and rolled to the floor. Paint bottles, brushes, inks, books, and other trinkets rained down. The last paint jar fell, then silence. He tore his gaze away and tossed the Webley— his father's gun, the only gun he'd ever trusted, but now the slayer of innocents, two by his own hand—onto the floor next to her.

"Bloody hell."

First Sadie. Now Therese. Then, under coercion, but now … because he'd no other choice. How many more? Because of him?

He coughed. "Heh. Survey says … none. Not going to be around long enough, see?" And there was a kind of mercy. One even he could accept.

His chest twisted. He gasped and coughed. His eyes hurt, head and heart pounded. He blinked, and the room tilted. He'd run out of time.

He staggered forward, determined to see it through to the end, before the darkness took him. With the protective ward almost gone, the Hive screamed in his mind. He knelt by Therese's fallen body. Shaking, he slipped his arms under her. He trembled with the strain as he lifted her and stood. Teetering, he thought for a moment he'd drop her.

He closed his eyes. "Dammit. I'm Hiram Grange. This is what I *do*."

With another breath came strength. Turning, he squared his shoulders and walked towards the fading ward. He stopped, scuffed a break in the chalk with his toe and whispered, "*Palasu*."

The ward dissolved. Cradling Therese close to his chest, he walked through the door and out into cries of hunger and delight.

Chapter Thirty-Four

Hiram shuffled forward. His chest burned. He felt the things wriggling inside him. Soon, they'd rip through his heart. He coughed up blood, spotting Therese's once-white sweater, now stained with blood and other fluids. He struggled to breathe, then realized with dismay—and some relief—he no longer could.

The hall narrowed. Blackness crept in. The things inside ripped and tore. He coughed up more blood, clotted and thick. It dribbled from his lips and nose. He weaved, almost crumpled against the wall. He dragged himself on.

I ... am ... Hiram Grange ... dammit.

One more step, into the lobby, where the monsters awaited. The Hive thrust itself into his mind, overwhelming his thoughts with their drone.

FEED!

He smiled. They wanted him because of how many he'd killed, but he'd show the slimy bastards. He'd die. That would fix them.

His heart twisted and he sagged to his knees. Therese rolled from his arms onto the floor. Something surged from his guts. He turned away from Therese and vomited black streams of bile.

Time.

He slumped among the other corpses. The lights winked out, one by one—like huge, old-fashioned but beautiful Christmas tree lights. Father had always complained those ancient things would set the house on fire someday.

Mother had loved them. So had he.

He shook, once. Something tore loose, deep inside. The keening of the hungry Tanara'ri faded. At least he'd fallen facing Therese; he saw nothing but her smooth, peaceful face.

Even that went away. Everything grayed, faded to snow white, then snapped to black. There was a rush of wind.

Hiram Grange died.

Chapter Thirty-Five

Therese stood in her nightmare hall and stared at the door she'd dreamed of her entire life. Its outline glowed with a bluish-white pulse, along with something else she'd never seen there before, etched in blazing white light: the sigil of Mab.

"You don't have to do this alone. I can show you how to use the power."

She turned, and once again faced The Chosen One.

"No one will accept you. Not humans, not Faerie, certainly not Mab." She nodded at the door, cobalt eyes squinting. "Not even Hiram. I'm *the only one* who can help you. I have generations of experience. I can teach you how to rule."

Therese glanced at the door. So much light poured from the burning sigil, so much power. "I don't want to rule," she whispered.

"But you will. It's unavoidable. It's your destiny."

The door flew open. The whitest light she'd ever seen surged out. It was cold and burning.

The Chosen One gripped her hand. "Don't worry. I'll be here, every step of the way."

T'herese sat up. Power blazed inside her. She knew everything: things as they were, and as they should be. Things were *not* as they should be. Darkness tainted all. It must be cleansed. Wrongs needed to be made right.

She sensed the dark things around her, things that had destroyed life. She plunged into their thoughts. They convulsed, tentacles snapping as she tore at their minds ...

"It's not enough," she whispered in an empty voice. "It's *never* enough."

She spread her arms and screamed. Rage filled the lobby, powered by the full tide of the white river, surging from her hands, spreading outward. All dark things vaporized in its wake.

She remembered the mangled corpses. They must be cleansed. She screamed again, but this time it was for *them*, the lingering dead, as they must've screamed. The lobby caught fire. Unnatural blue-white flames ignited the corpses and ruined bodies, cleansing them. Fire danced along the floor and ceiling and walls. It burnt *away* the stains of darkness.

Other vile things lurked, waiting to feed. She reached into the Hive and destroyed them wherever they were.

It *still* wasn't enough. "Hiram," she murmured.

She grabbed him by the lapels of his tattered, blood-soaked suit and poured the white river into him. "Hiram … *come back!*"

Power pulsed into him; his arms flopped and legs twitched. Dead eyes opened and irises swelled, but he did not breathe. Wherever he was … *would not let go.*

"*HIRAM!!!!*"

She blasted into the air, dragging Hiram's still lifeless corpse with her. Her power surged and reached a crescendo as she held him close. Throwing her head back, she screamed, releasing it all.

"*HIRAMMMMMMMMMMMMMMMM!*"

Everything above the lobby vaporized. As she spun higher, the white fire flowed outward. Therese struggled loose of The Chosen One's grip long enough to whisper into Hiram's ear. "P-please. Hiram. Come back! I can't control it … can't control her …!"

The Chosen One shoved Therese Fitzgerald aside and bellowed. The world trembled.

Earthquakes rocked California, Zimbabwe and Japan.

A deluge flooded the Sudan. A class five hurricane struck Florida. Angry snows and hail pummeled Maine, Massachusetts and New Hampshire.

The world spasmed as the white river pulsed out to purify ... *everything*.

"Hmmm. Interesting."

All things considered, Hiram hadn't expected this. He'd imagined the Abyss differently: madness, pain, fire, even brimstone, not a deserted crossroads surrounded by a dark forest.

"Well. Who would've thought hell would be so damned ... abstract. I was expecting at the very least legions of the dead with ten-foot flames as backdrops." He shook his head. "I'm disappointed, quite frankly."

This isn't hell.

He looked around, then yelped when someone tugged his elbow. Turning, he saw what appeared to be a teenage boy in jeans and a white T-shirt. His eyes blazed bright blue.

"This *isn't* hell."

He nodded. "You're right, of course. Hell would be a Kenny G concert with no exits."

He flashed a wide smile, which faltered as the boy gazed back at him, expressionless. He kicked the ground and scowled. "Kali's tit. Does *everyone* hate my jokes this much?" He shook his head. "If this isn't hell, what is it?"

The boy tipped his head, brow furrowed. "A way station. A place for decisions."

"Decisions? About what?"

"About many things."

"Well, *that's* specific. So why am *I* here?"

The boy pursed his lips. "You have to stop her."

"Who? Therese?"

"Yes. She's *Becoming*. Gathering the White River into her, to release upon the world." A dreadful pause hung. "You must stop her."

The irony killed him. "Unbelievable. Even here, it continues: 'Hiram, do this ... Hiram, do that.'" He shook his head. "Why should I?"

The boy didn't answer. The silence grew, so he turned, said more forcibly, "Seriously—why? Better question ... how?"

The boy looked away. "By showing her what she's destroying. By showing her love."

"Oh *hell*. How very *Hallmark*. Listen, I don't mean to insult your omnipotence ... but you do know who you're talking to, right?"

The boy turned his burning gaze upon him. It cleaved his protests in two. "You *have* loved."

His gut twisted, felt brittle. "Right. Look how well *that* turned out."

"You persevere."

"Shit." He waved him away. "I don't know *why*, though. Certainly not because I'm any good. At least Mother had the courage to pull the trigger. I haven't even got that."

"And yet ... you continue."

He closed his eyes, relishing the blackness. Something trembled inside. "Can't I just stay here? I'm so damn ... *tired*. Of everything."

"Hiram."

The voice softened. He opened his eyes and stared. Where the boy had stood was now the patchwork woman from his dreams. This being was stitched together—with luminous threads—from only two women.

Sadie and Mother.

Hiram stepped back, overwhelmed. "No. *No.*"

The being moved closer, imploring with her hands. "It's not your time, Hiram. You have too much to do. A *destiny* to fulfill."

"You mean like Mab's visions? Hell …"

"Prophecies never work as they seem, Hiram. You *don't* have to become what you hate."

"No." He looked at his feet, feeling small, weak. "I can't do this. I don't know what to say. I could never talk to either of you. How can I now?"

The patchwork woman took his face into her hands. Unlike Therese's, hers throbbed with warmth. "Don't speak, Hiram. *Show her.* Show her what we should've shown you, long ago.

"*Show her.*"

Chapter Thirty-Six

... show her.

Hiram gasped. Fire burnt his lungs. A massive tug hauled him upwards. Every nerve in his body thrummed as the energies of the Veil pulsed through him. Spinning into the air, he touched *everything* through Therese—hate and love and envy and fear and joy and sadness, madness and grief and hope and despair. In a heartbeat, he felt it all.

"P-please. Hiram, *come back!* I can't control her ... can't control it ...!"

I don't know what to say ...

Show her.

Hiram worked his arms free as they spun higher. Power throbbed and crackled all around. He felt it in her touch: a threshold had been reached. A great tide rose inside her.

Show her.

Hiram clasped Therese's face and kissed her. Reaching down to the darkest parts of his soul, he pulled the memories—thoughts, pictures, feelings—of Mother and of Sadie, flooded his mind with them, sent them to Therese. Arousal, excitement, fear ... and desire; sparked by the taste of her on his tongue. Their bodies pressed together, and as Hiram allowed every bit of sadness and grief to surface, he found something else there. Love. Hope. Peace.

The Chosen One fought back, but he let his memories and passions flow, relentless. Every ounce of his pain, but with that torment, undeniable moments of happiness, pleasure, wistfulness. His hands slipped to the small of Therese's back, pressed her hips to his as their kiss deepened. His thin frame melded with hers, her soft curves molded over his hard angles.

Therese pressed back, tasting his tongue, his mouth, *his life*. She reached up, cradled his head in her hands, accepting all that he gave.

The Chosen One screamed. The universe convulsed as Hiram felt something ripple between them, something deeper and more fundamental than a mere orgasm could possibly be, but *that's what it was*—a cresting, a breaching—as he and Therese reached a crescendo …

… and exploded.

Chapter Thirty-Seven

*T*herese grasped the doorknob. It throbbed with power ... but she no longer felt so afraid.

She glanced over her shoulder. The Chosen One stood, arms crossed, looking almost petulant. "You'll never survive without me. You're a fool."

Therese smiled. "I suppose that'll have to do."

The Chosen One cracked her neck, rolled her shoulders and relaxed, suddenly smug. "I'm glad we had this chat. We'll do it again ... very soon."

Therese frowned. "Don't hold your breath, sweetheart."

"Funny. That's not 'no' ... is it?" A pause. "See you soon, dear."

Therese didn't respond. Filled with a curious mixture of hope, dread, and fierce certainty, she opened the door and walked into the shining world beyond

Chapter Thirty-Eight

A Week Later – Jimmy's

James Conlon appraised the new counter in his bar with satisfaction. The old one hadn't been damaged in last week's row—not like his front window and the bathroom—but what the hell, right? It had been rundown enough. He'd wanted to replace the eyesore for a while now. Because the fight had wrecked his old place, his insurance had allowed him to upgrade. It was on the shady side of legal, but he knew a constable or two. He'd greased the wheels with waived tabs. No one seemed wiser.

"Excuse me ... which *Bushmills* do you have in stock?"

Conlon jerked and stared at the sharp, angular features: awkward cutting nose, intense eyes. He opened his mouth, but nothing came out save a high-pitched squeak as he recognized the outdated and ill-fitting cut of the man's suit.

The man frowned. "Hell, mate. You all right? Looks like someone stepped on your grave."

Conlon looked for at least one friendly constable to have the man arrested, or at least run off. He found none.

"Whatever you want, " he muttered, looking down into his hands, avoiding the man's gaze. He grabbed a fresh bottle of *Bushmills 21 Year* from the wall behind and slid it across the bar. "On the house." Giving the counter a few hurried, token swipes with a rag, he shambled away.

"What the hell is *his* problem?" muttered a vexed Hiram Grange. He twisted the cork from the bottle and grabbed a glass from the bar.

"Probably worried you'll trash his place again," murmured a voice of silken-steel over his shoulder. "You know—that maybe you'll set it on fire, this time."

Hiram turned to face Mab. Dressed in a simple—and positively tasty—black, full-body leather suit under a demure duster, she blended in with the crowd. Hair pulled into a plain ponytail, feet shod in thigh-high leather boots, Mab looked like a biker-girl cruising for action. As always, Hiram swatted down a pleasurable heat. This was Mab, after all.

Pity.

"Mab." He leaned on the bar. "You look positively Hell's Angelish. Got your *Harley* parked outside?"

Mab raised an eyebrow. "You look well yourself. Much better than I expected, actually."

He smirked. "And look—all human. No world destroying powers."

"Visions don't work that way. Still plenty of time for it to come true."

Hiram slowly poured himself a glass of the amber whiskey, took a healthy gulp before responding. "Sorry to disappoint, Mab, but no apocalypses forthcoming here. Talked with the Big Man himself. Got it all worked out."

She tilted her head. "What *are* you talking about?"

"The Big Man? Big Kahuna? You know ... God? Well, he looked like a twelve-year-old boy, but I'm pretty sure he was God, or someone else important, cosmologically speaking."

"Please. You were near death, Therese dragged you back from it, and you hallucinated."

"See, that's the problem with being a messiah. No one ever believes in you until it's too late."

Mab stiffened. "What do you mean by *that?*"

He made a face. "Bloody hell, Mab. It's a joke."

"Hiram, listen ..."

And suddenly, he reached his limit. "No, you listen to *me*, you manipulative little bitch. You used me; *again*. I don't exactly know how, but you did."

Mab's face assumed an expression of studied indifference. "I don't know what you're talking about."

He snorted. "Please. Don't patronize me. This whole thing reeks. It did from the start."

"How do you mean?"

"Whoever summoned the Tanara'ri didn't want revenge against the Faerie. No mortal has that power, knows how to construct such a Binding. Someone had to have instructed them. Someone from your domain, or somewhere like it. This whole thing was about Therese. They knew who she was; knew how powerful her flat's aura would be. There's simply too much premeditation here: Binding the Tanara'ri to her, forcing her to manifest, summoning the Tanara'ri with your sigil."

Mab said nothing. Arms crossed, her cobalt blue eyes burned into his. Hiram ignored her and continued. "You know what occurred to me while I was recovering? You said Therese's powers were Bound, and that if I didn't do something soon she'd break that Binding. I assumed you meant a magical binding. Then I remembered what you said about enthralling the poor blokes who fathered the scions, that—even though you'd no idea why—magic couldn't be involved. The whole thing had to be pure."

He straightened. "Her Binding wasn't magic; it was her humanity. When I killed her, I broke her Binding. And the funny thing is, I think you told me to do it."

At this, Mab scowled. "You've *no* idea what you're saying."

Hiram smiled. If there was one thing he enjoyed, it was watching arrogant people squirm. "Words are funny, Mab. When first spoken, their true meanings are often missed. While resting and composing my thoughts, something occurred to me: your words about Therese, and what I needed to do. They were very oddly phrased, when you think about it; such highbrow statements as: 'destroy the vessel, loose the power of the Veil.'" He smirked. "Call me insane, but not once did you actually say: 'Kill Therese.' You certainly said, 'She must die,' but you never said, 'kill her.'"

"This is nonsense." Mab shifted her weight. Her anger and defensiveness had dissipated, replaced by her usual brand of smug superiority. "I hope you feel very satisfied with all your posturing, but ..."

"Mab, listen very carefully. I never want to see you again ... ever. Not even if space-time is unraveling, or if Faerie's sacred line of Welsh poodles is threatening to destroy the natural order. All jesting aside about who can kick who's ass; if I see you again ... *I'll kill you.*"

He stared at Mab for several long seconds. It occurred to him that he'd made a habit of pissing on the shoes of very powerful beings, but he'd never been a study in social graces. Why change now?

Seconds passed. Mab nodded and turned to leave, only to face Therese.

The moment hung. As Hiram watched them face off, the air filled with ambient energy. Surrounding patrons must have felt it, for several of them glanced at the simmering contest, though they probably assumed it was over something mundane, his affections, perhaps.

The thought gave him much pleasure.

The standoff lasted several more seconds. He was struck even more so by the similarity in their features. Therese looked like Mab's younger cousin, or even sister.

Slowly, the tension faded. He saw Mab force herself to relax. "We'll be watching," she whispered. "Closely."

Therese remained silent a second longer, then flashed Mab a luminous smile that dispelled the Faerie Queen's coldness. "Don't wait up, *Mum*."

The look on Mab's face was priceless. She hesitated a beat, then without another word pushed past Therese, bumping shoulders.

Therese continued to smile as she approached Hiram. Dressed much like she was the night he'd first seen her, in a simple white blouse and skirt, though this time wearing a brown leather jacket, she looked like an average college girl, out to stretch her legs.

She leaned on the bar, affecting his pose, and watched Mab's departure. "You know, I've always dreamed of meeting my birth mother someday. Wondered what she was like, if we'd get on; that sort of thing." She offered him a grin. "Turns out, the experience is vastly overrated."

He smiled. "Well, that's Mab; she of the eternally twisted panties. You'll get used to her."

Therese tossed her hair and chuckled, a gesture he found endearing ... and utterly normal. "Nice jacket. New?"

Therese's smile faded. "No. It's Reggie's, actually. I went over to his place today to collect a few things. Thought I'd keep this ... to remind me."

Something inside him twisted, thinking of the countless Jodie Foster collages at home. "Looks good on you. Fits well."

"Thanks. So ... did your Bothwell ever discover who's behind all this?"

"No. None of her leads panned out. The University's vice-provost—Stemmins—turned out to be a rather mundane, run-of-the-mill dodgy bastard in the end. Only thing Bothwell uncovered: the custodian for your dormitory, a Julian Williams, has disappeared. He'd been living with his grandmother. They found her dead of a presumed heart attack in her flat. Someone cleaned out her bank accounts, though. A week ago. And, among his things they found several old spell books, arcane volumes ... though none of them contained a spell for the Binding found in your apartment."

Therese looked thoughtful. "God. Makes sense. He had keys to everything, didn't he? I don't even know what he looked like, although

I must've … had to have bumped into him at some point …"

"Don't sell yourself short. No one else could remember exactly what he looked like, either. Man like that would've been adept at moving around unnoticed. Also, probably used a Glamor—a spell to cloud his face—so even if you *had* spoken to him directly, you'd still forget his face."

"I suppose. Are you off, then?"

He nodded. "Bothwell needs me in London. Hellhounds, I believe. Nasty brutes … but at least they don't replicate like demonized bunnies, have horrid, leathery tentacles and all those blasted eyes."

Therese shook her head. "Hellhounds, tentacled monsters …" She smiled. "The world you live in, Hiram Grange. Mind-boggling."

He grinned. "*I* was going to say absolutely dreadful, but thanks. Besides, it's also *your* world now. Welcome to it."

She nodded, her face sobering. In most ways, he didn't envy her. She had much to unravel. As far he was concerned, he'd done enough unraveling. It was time to get back to the simple life of pointing loud guns at nasty things, pulling the trigger, and making them go away.

He chuckled. *The simple life, indeed.* "So, I imagine you'll be on your way?"

She inclined her head, looked thoughtful and a bit sad. "Yes. This wonderful new world of yours is absolutely *thrilling*. But if it's all the same, I'd like to leave it behind for a while."

"Understandable. You know, if you happen out East, there's a secluded enclave of Tibetan monks who proved very hospitable to me several years back, when I rid their village of a wendigo …" At her furrowed brows, he gestured a hand over his head, "Big furry white beast, somewhat like a yeti, about so high? Anyway, I didn't stay with them very long …" He flashed a rueful grin, "Not nearly enough women there to suit my tastes, but I imagine that you'd appreciate the quiet. They're not the Faerie—*thankfully*—but if there's anyone who can teach you balance, it's them."

Therese sighed and nodded. She looked around the crowded pub. "Sounds like an idea. I've got so much to think about."

"Such as?"

"About what to do next." There was silence, until she added, "I've always wanted mutually exclusive things, I think. Just to be normal, but also to be special." She glanced at him sidelong, smirking. "Of course, now that I have *one* ... I think all I really want is the *other*. Ironic, isn't it?"

"They say fate is a harsh mistress. If that's the case, then irony is her bitchy little sister." They both shared a laugh.

Therese sobered as she caught the evening news on a television mounted over the bar. It still told the story of last week's terrible "terrorist" attack at University Quarter, calling the dead "brave heroes." Now they were giving an update about a group that had been uncovered, believed responsible.

"No one knows, do they?" She looked at him, eyes wide and glistening. "About the things you do? The battles you fight."

For a moment, he'd no answer. Then he said, "*We* know, Therese. Most nights, that's enough. And when it's not, I drink far too much and sleep with many strange women. All at the same time. It evens out in the end."

Therese shook her head, lips caught between a frown and a smile. "You're incorrigible."

"That's what Bothwell says. Frankly, I think she's jealous." They fell into a companionable silence, both knowing what must come next, neither wanting it.

Eventually, Therese sighed and gave him a lopsided grin. "I suppose words would cheapen the whole thing, wouldn't they?"

"True. But we're human, so we're bound to try, anyway."

She held out her hand. "In that case ... thank you. For everything."

He smiled—which, unfortunately, he sensed would happen far less often without Therese around—and returned her handshake, amazed at the subtle strength gripping his hand. "And thank you, also."

"Well, I'm off then. Like I said … much thinking to do."

"When's your flight?"

"Whenever I want, actually. One of the benefits … I run my own flight plans, now."

"I should think so. Take care, then. Try to avoid destroying the world, if you could. Might interfere with my schedule."

She flashed him a wide smile, though he saw shades of icy cobalt flickering in her eyes. "I'll get right on that." With another nod, she walked away. Three steps later—at that exact moment when a person merges with a crowd —she faded into wisps of whitish-blue vapor and disappeared.

His gaze lingered there. Again, he was as he'd always been: alone.

He thought of Sadie. She wouldn't have wanted this for him. Not at all. He decided that when he got back to the States, he'd procure copious amounts of absinthe, drink until he couldn't stand, then while recovering, select Sadie's finest Jodie collage, frame it, and destroy the rest.

He'd still hurt. No changing that.

He was, however, Hiram Grange. Hurting was what he did best.

Turning back to the bar, he noticed a young lady sitting at his elbow who looked barely nineteen. Hair dyed pitch-black, both eyebrows and her upper lip pierced with emerald-green studs; she was to his eyes like water to a man dying of thirst. She wore tight leather pants hitched low enough to see the top of her lime green thong, and a black mesh shirt over … well, not much at all.

He tipped his head, caught her eye … and saw something flicker there. She returned his gaze and gave him a slow, sensuous smile—absolutely wicked on such a young mouth. She raised a studded eyebrow, but before he could speak, she said, "Name's Lilith. Share that drink? Or is an old man like you used up for the night?"

As he grabbed a fresh glass from the bar and began to pour, something very tight inside him uncoiled after far too long. "Hiram. My name is Hiram Grange, and I believe my night has just begun."

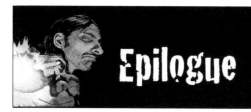

Epilogue

Mab entered an office that had no substance in reality. In many ways, its genesis was a mystery to her. That shouldn't be. She was Mab, Queen of Faerie. Nothing in the universe should be hidden from her.

As she approached what appeared to be a wide, antique mahogany desk, a small part of her quivered. The office's mystery was the least of her worries. The person sitting behind the desk? Far worse.

She stopped, clasped her hands behind her back, and assumed a regal pose. "It is done. Our contract is dissolved. You have no further claim upon me."

He Who Walks In White smiled, teeth gleaming. He puttered with a papery-white object—what looked like an origami creature of some sort—and said, "Indeed. You've done well, much better than I expected, actually." Outwardly he seemed congenial, but she knew better. His eyes glittered with a festering blackness that made the little girl inside her—the child she'd thought long since banished with her ascension—tremble.

A few more folds and he made a satisfied noise. "It's amazing how much of the universe is layered in coincidence. Who would've thought that a desperate little girl, who sold her soul to escape an orphanage where she was raped daily, was also a scion who'd someday ascend to Faerie? And who would've thought that contract would still be binding after her ascension?"

He chuckled. "I have to admit, that was a calculated risk on my part. Didn't know how it would play out, or if I'd even have need of such an arrangement. Just goes to show the pleasant unexpectedness of order hiding within chaos."

Mab's teeth ground at his dismissive tone, but she repressed her anger. As powerful as she was, this ... *thing* ... was an unknown. She'd no idea of his capabilities. Still, she couldn't repress curiosity. "I don't understand. You failed. Therese didn't become The Destroyer, and Hiram appears no worse for wear, back to his irritating self."

His smile held hidden menace and was all teeth. "Poor Mab. The Faerie know so much, but they still understand so little about human nature. That's the wonderful thing about humans, Mab: free will. The Faerie have a semblance of free will, but you're tied to the universe's natural order; tied to the Veil, tied to your own contracts and bargains. Can't even lie, can you? Only misdirect and mislead through vague wordplay. Even this betrayal of yours was only possible through the pledge you made with me."

Reverently, he placed the completed origami, a delicately folded dragon, on the desk, sat forward and folded his hands. "Humans, though ... well, there's an insane beauty in their free will. They break promises, go back on their word, change their minds, whenever they damn well please ... if they're prodded hard enough. Therese? She's made a decision, yes. That means nothing. Few human decisions remain absolute. And Grange? He died and was resurrected by the Veil itself. That sort of thing changes a fellow ... forever." Something about his manner grew cold, his friendly visage stiffening for a moment into something more predatory. "I should know."

Mab swallowed, fought to keep her face impassive. "I'm done with this. I've fulfilled our pact. You've no hold on me, now."

"This is true, which is a problem." One hand disappeared and pulled open an unseen drawer. "You're a loose end now, aren't you? Can't have that."

With a swiftness that surprised even her, He Who Walks In White pointed a pistol of indeterminate design at her. "Luckily for me," he murmured, "Bothwell's idea of crafting iron bullets wasn't all that original. And don't try to leave. The inner door is also coated in iron, which I'm sure you noticed as soon it closed."

She bit her lip. She had, of course. Her legs had trembled in weakness as soon as the door swung shut. By then ... it had been too late.

"Goodbye, Mab." He thumbed back the safety.

Mab's eyes widened in horror.

KEVIN LUCIA

KEVIN LUCIA is a Contributing Editor for *Shroud Magazine*. His short fiction has appeared in several anthologies. He teaches high school English, and is working on a Creative Writing Masters Degree at Binghamton University. He lives in Castle Creek, New York with his wife and children. He is also currently writing his first full-length novel.

Visit Kevin online at *www.kevinlucia.net*.

THE SCANDALOUS MISADVENTURES OF

BOOK 1

Jake Burrows

Hiram Grange & the Village of the Damned

Something wicked walks the streets of the picturesque New Hampshire village of Great Bay—something that has inexplicably risen from the grave to wreak a horrifying vengeance. Only one man can stop it—Hiram Grange—provided he can sober up long enough to answer the call!

BOOK 2

Scott Christian Carr

Hiram Grange & the Twelve Little Hitlers

Hitler has escaped. Twelve of them, to be precise, each cloned from the original, and hiding in the bizarre American underground. Hiram Grange has been tasked with hunting them down. The only problem: he's hit rock bottom. His worst binge ever— a mad dance with absinthe, opium and depression …

BOOK 3

Robert Davies

Hiram Grange & the Digital Eucharist

From its global headquarters in Boston, the mysterious Occlusionist Movement is preparing to control the world with its Digital Eucharist, while in the serpentine bowels of the city an ancient demon is unleashed, eager for revenge against the man who imprisoned it years ago—Hiram Grange!

HIRAM GRANGE

BOOK 4
Kevin Lucia
Hiram Grange & the Chosen One
Hiram Grange doesn't believe in fate. He makes his own destiny. That's a good thing, because Queen Mab of Faerie has foreseen the destruction of the world, and as usual ... it's all Hiram's fault. He must choose: kill an innocent girl and save the universe ... or rescue her and watch all else burn.
Just another day on the job for Hiram Grange.

BOOK 5
Richard Wright
Hiram Grange & the Nymphs of Krakow
Hiram Grange was already broken when his world was turned upside down by the horrifying revelations of a beautiful and dangerous woman. Faced with the possibility that he's been a pawn in a diabolical game, he seeks the truth in the snows of Krakow. But the truth is guarded by ancient, winged things, and the truth has teeth ...

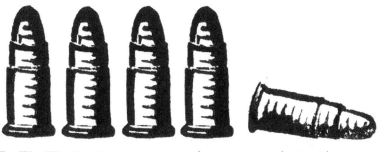

WWW.HIRAMGRANGE.COM

Also from Shroud Publishing ...

Maurice Broaddus • *Devil's Marionette*

Death comes for the cast and crew of the hit comedy TV Show Chocolate City, impacting not only their personal lives but the prospect of their show's continued success. As each member sinks into their own past, and the spirits of those that came before, the tragedies continue.

When your terror comes to claim you, who will it be? *Nobody*.

R. Scott McCoy • *FEAST*

Deputy Sheriff Nick Ambrose can look into someone's eyes and glimpse their guilt, to an extent. But when he and his brother take on a psychopathic killer, he gains something more: the ability to see, and devour, souls. Plagued by this terrifying new power, and by the spirits of both his brother and the butcher trapped inside his mind, he sets out to understand and control his new fate and to grapple with the shadowy auras he now sees all around.

Can he command the darkness welling within, or will he become merely its vessel?

Cindy Little • *Intruder*

When the powers of an ancient malevolent creature invade a quiet suburban household, a young mother is forced into a pitched battle for the life of her child.

Rio Youers • *Mama Fish*

At Harlequin High School In 1986, Kelvin Fish is the oddball, the weird kid that no one will talk to, except for Patrick Beauchamp, who is determined to learn more. When Patrick's curiosity leads him into a bizarre and tragic series of events, he gets much more than he bargained for.

D. Harlan Wilson • *Peckinpah: An Ultraviolent Romance*

Life in Dreamfield is a daily harangue of pigs, cornfields, pigs, fast food joints, pigs, Dollar Stores, pigs, motorcycles, pigs, and good old-fashioned Amerikan redneckery. Angry, slick-talking, and ultraviolent to the core, Samson Thataway and the Fuming Garcias commit art-for-art's-sake in the form of hideous, unmotivated serial killings. When an unsuspecting everyman's wife is murdered by the throng, it is up to Felix Soandso to avenge her death and return Dreamfield to its natural state of absurdity.

SHROUD Magazine

Published quarterly, SHROUD contains the latest pulse-pounding stories from the masters of the genre. Fiction, art, book reviews, films, and insightful articles that pull back the veil separating fantasy from reality. Shocking, cerebral and satisfying.

Available now at www.shroudmagazine.com

Made in the USA
Lexington, KY
29 May 2010